W9-CEU-697

SHADOW BEAR

SHADOW BEAR

Lakota

CASSIE EDWARDS

WHEELER
CHIVERS

This Large Print edition is published by Wheeler Publishing, Waterville, Maine, USA and by BBC Audiobooks Ltd, Bath, England.
Wheeler Publishing is an imprint of The Gale Group.
Wheeler is a trademark and used herein under license.

ALL RIGHTS RESERVED

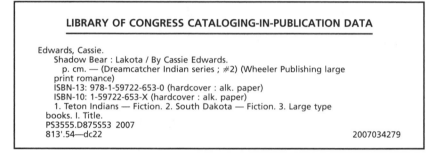

LIBRARY OF CONGRESS CATALOGING-IN-PUBLICATION DATA

Edwards, Cassie.
    Shadow Bear : Lakota / By Cassie Edwards.
        p. cm. — (Dreamcatcher Indian series ; #2) (Wheeler Publishing large print romance)
    ISBN-13: 978-1-59722-653-0 (hardcover : alk. paper)
    ISBN-10: 1-59722-653-X (hardcover : alk. paper)
    1. Teton Indians — Fiction. 2. South Dakota — Fiction. 3. Large type books. I. Title.
PS3555.D875S53 2007
813'.54—dc22   2007034279

BRITISH LIBRARY CATALOGUING-IN-PUBLICATION DATA AVAILABLE

Published in 2007 in the U.S. by arrangement with NAL Signet, a member of Penguin Group (USA) Inc.
Published in 2008 in the U.K. by arrangement with Penguin Group (USA) Inc.

U.K. Hardcover: 978 1 405 64332 0 (Chivers Large Print)
U.K. Softcover: 978 1 405 64333 7 (Camden Large Print)

Printed in the United States of America on permanent paper
10 9 8 7 6 5 4 3 2 1

I am dedicating *Shadow Bear* to two very special sweet friends and fans — Ida Morehouse and Dorothy Lewis.
  You are appreciated!

Love,
Cassie

DREAM CATCHER

Oh, dream catcher,
Will you catch this beautiful dream,
Hold it safe from my eyes unseen?
Oh, dream catcher,
Is it really true,
That I am that eagle soaring across skies so
    blue?
Oh, dream catcher,
I am that mother bear,
Fighting, surviving, guarding against those
here and there.
Oh, dream catcher,
Catch the dreams of my heart,
Keep them there.

                    — Mordestia M. York

CHAPTER 1

The breeze is whispering in the bush,
And the leaves fall from the tree,
All sighing on, and will not hush,
Some pleasant tales of thee.
— John Clare

Moon When the Ponies Shed — May
South Dakota, 1850

The sky was blue, the sun hidden beneath a cluster of darkening clouds. The tepee flaps were lifted throughout the Lakota village so that the midmorning breeze could waft into the lodges to help cool the interiors.

Chief Shadow Bear, a young warrior of twenty-five winters, of the Gray Owl Band of the Lakota tribe, sat with his *unci,* grandmother, Dancing Breeze, in his personal tepee.

The frown on his grandmother's face

9

proved that she had not come this morning with news that was pleasant, or *wasteste,* good.

As Shadow Bear waited for her to tell him what was troubling her, he gazed at a woman of many winters. The tightly drawn flesh across her cheekbones proved again to Shadow Bear how much she had wasted away from despair. Two months ago she had mourned the death of both her chieftain husband and her son, who was Shadow Bear's *ahte,* father.

On that fateful day, Shadow Bear's *ina,* mother, had also died, and all because of a mistaken identity. Their white buffalo hunter assailants mistook them for their enemies from a different band of Lakota. When they discovered their mistake, the buffalo hunters fled into the hills and had not been seen since, so they could not pay for their crimes.

When news had spread to Shadow Bear's village, and the bodies of those who had been slain arrived home for their burial rites, many weeks of mourning had begun. But before they started, Shadow Bear had acquired the title of chief in place of his fallen chieftain grandfather.

Ho, yes, his grandmother had mourned since, having lost a husband and son on the same day. But today it seemed she had come from her private lodge to share something with Shadow Bear that had put fear in her sunken and aged dark eyes.

Shadow Bear sat before cold ashes in his fire pit wearing only a brief, cool breechclout. His weasel-wrapped braids hung long over his broad shoulders, where a necklace of beads lay against his smooth skin.

His grandmother sat opposite the fire pit from him, quiet and withdrawn. Shadow Bear could not help but be wary of what she was about to tell him, because she had the power of *Wakinyan,* the power of great intuition, and the ability to foretell events.

Her wiry gray hair hung in one long braid down her narrow, bent back. Her heavily beaded doeskin dress was loose upon a body that was more bone now than flesh.

She was quiet for so long that Shadow Bear knew what she was about to tell him was not good.

"Grandmother, why have you come to my lodge today?" Shadow Bear blurted out, his patience having run thin. "What is it I see in your eyes that I cannot help but be troubled about?"

"My *mitakoza,* grandson, I have seen a great *peta,* fire, in my visions," she finally said in an old, gruff voice that sounded more like a man's now that she had entered

11

her eightieth year of life.

"But I see our people spared because they are clever enough to prepare in time for the fire," she then said.

"And in your vision what did you see our people do in order not to be touched by such a fire?" Shadow Bear asked.

He was trying not to show his alarm over the news . . . which he knew would turn into reality, for his grandmother's visions were never wrong.

"My *mitakoza,* grandson, you will instruct our people about my vision, as well as instruct them how to prepare for what it foretells, so that none of our village lodges fall beneath the hot flames of fire," Dancing Breeze said tightly. "You will tell them to prepare for the fire by digging a great, wide trench on the vulnerable sides of our village, as well as our communal garden. There are only two sides of our village that are unprotected, where the digging must be done. The other two are protected by the great river that makes a sharp bend in the land on those two sides."

Shadow Bear saw tears shine suddenly in her old eyes. "And what else did you see, Grandmother, in your visions, that makes you ready to cry?" he asked thickly, believing he already knew.

12

His brother, her other grandson, Silent Arrow, surely was the cause.

After their warriors' recent successful hunt, Shadow Bear's brother, Silent Arrow, had been chosen to take the finest of the tanned and decorated robes to the top of a hill. They left the robes there as a gift of gratitude offered to their brother the buffalo, because so many of the buffalos' relations had died to feed the Lakota, who would in their turn die and feed the grasses that would then feed the buffalo.

His brother should have arrived home by now, his sacred deed successfully done.

"I also saw your brother, Silent Arrow, in a vision," Dancing Breeze said, her voice breaking with emotion. "He is in trouble, Shadow Bear, or he would have returned home by now."

"*Ho,* yes, *hecitu-yelow,* that is true. He should have," Shadow Bear said. "I had decided to go search for him after our talk."

"*Hoye,* that is good," Dancing Breeze said, slowly nodding her head. "I knew that you would be as concerned as I and go and search for him."

She wiped away tears with her old, bony fingers, then gazed more intensely into Shadow Bear's eyes. "*Iho.* Go. Instruct our people to begin digging the trench and then

13

leave immediately thereafter to search for your brother. But be careful, my grandson. Do not allow yourself to get caught and trapped amid the flames of the fire."

She pushed herself slowly up from the bulrush mats that were spread across the floor. "I must go now to pray and hope for the best for our people and that my grandson will soon be among us once again," she said, her voice drawn.

Shadow Bear was quickly there to help her, his arm around her waist as he held her steady while walking her toward the raised entrance flap.

She turned her eyes up to his. "Please hurry, Shadow Bear, and do these things before it is too late," she said, her voice unsteady. "In my vision, I also saw the fields of sunflowers that are beloved by our Lakota people all scorched, the flowers no longer able to reach their faces toward the sun. I saw buffalo trapped amid flames."

She paused, swallowed hard, then said, "The sunflower and buffalo are two beloved symbols of our Lakota people. The sun is essential to all health and life. In spring, summer, and winter, rays are welcome. In the spring, its warmth brings forth new grass; in summer its heat cures the skins, dries the meat, and preserves food for storage. The buffalo are all and everything to the existence of the Lakota."

Her voice broke as she looked into her grandson's eyes with a strange sort of desperation. "In my vision I saw many *ptagica,* buffalo, die amid the flames," she said. She stepped outside with Shadow Bear. "Our people cannot stand losing many more buffalo, especially by a needless fire. The white man has already taken too many of them from us."

She turned to him and gently placed her hands on his cheeks. "You, our people's leader, have much to do," she said. "Do it."

He smiled down at her, took her hands gently from his face, then walked her to her own private tepee.

Shadow Bear swept his arms around his grandmother. He gave her a gentle hug, then held the entrance flap aside so that she could go inside the privacy of her lodge.

Then, knowing what must be done, he turned and gazed at his people, who were yet to know the trouble that lay before them.

He looked slowly around him at the peace of his village. He hated casting a shadow of doom over them all, and for the moment soaked in the wondrous sight that could be lost if they did not prepare carefully.

Some of his people's younger braves sat in

a circle playing the plum-pit game. Else-where, some older men sat cross-legged in a circle in the shade of the lodges that, like his own, were rolled up around the edges to coax the whirlwinds through. They moved their eagle-wing fans slowly, the red willow bark in their pipes fragrant on the air.

Shadow Bear watched several women dressed in their doeskin working dresses coming in with their wicker baskets piled high with various fruits. This was the most welcome season of the year . . . their fruit season.

Chokeberries, grapes, plums, currants, strawberries, and gooseberries grew plentiful in the woods and alongside the river and streams.

One of the first fruits to ripen was the *wazu-steca,* strawberries.

Then the wild plums would ripen and fall to the ground. The women would gather them, dry them, and put them in storage for winter food.

Later, in the fall, after the first frost, the fruit of the wild rose would turn red and make a delicious food, sweet raw or cooked.

The Lakota also gathered one plant that was not classified as a fruit. The bulrush, a tall plant that lived in the marshes in the early spring and summer, could be pulled up by the roots, and the white part eaten by his people like the white man's vegetable called celery.

Finding it hard to interfere in the peace and calm of his people today, Shadow Bear hesitated a while longer and enjoyed watching what his people were doing.

Some other women were occupied tending to the meat and skins that had recently been brought in by the successful warriors' hunt.

Racks hung heavy and ripe with fresh meat. While the meat dried hard and thin for the winter parfleche cases, the women took the hides to the stream to soak and treat them.

The space around some lodges was covered with skins stretching, flesh side up, the women scraping them, shaving them thin, and rubbing them with tallow and brains and other soft parts mixed together.

When these were dry, they would be stacked in piles in their lodges. Soon there would be many fine lodges there, newly painted with figures picturing the dreaming and deeds of their husbands who lived there. If the fire could be halted in time.

Knowing that he must not delay any longer, Shadow Bear stepped into the center of the village and drew all attention his way.

Everyone stopped what they were doing to hear what their chief had to say. He told them about what his grandmother had warned, and issued instructions on what they were to do.

Some were to dig.

Some were to bring in the horses.

And some were to bring in green grass in bundles for their horses, gathered from the damp places of the bordering streams.

"My people, remember that the soil in our village and surrounding it has absorbed the flesh and blood of our ancestors," Shadow Bear said solemnly as all listened intently. "We must save it from the big fire of my grandmother's vision."

He swallowed hard. "I cannot join you with the preparations," he said, trying to hide the emotion in his voice. "As you all know, my brother, Silent Arrow, has not returned home yet from his mission. I must go and find him and bring him safely back home before the fire erupts. I will search while you do your duties."

Everyone nodded and then hurried away to begin their tasks. After Shadow Bear had slid his rifle into the gun boot at the side of his horse and slapped a sheathed knife around his waist, he mounted the snow-white stallion he had named Star because of a dark spot above the eyes in the shape of a star.

He rode from the village, a sadness grabbing at his heart. After a while he saw several buffalo wandering through a field of sunflowers, lolling their heads as they walked. Loving the sunflowers so much, some of the animals had uprooted the plants and had wound them about their necks, letting sprays dangle from their horns.

It was a sight to behold, and he wished that he knew of a way to warn both the buffalo and the flowers of the upcoming tragedy that would soon unfold around them, but all that he could do was ride onward, soon leaving the peaceful sight behind him.

As he continued, he was reminded of just how dry of a spring it had been. Although the grass was young, for the most part, it was brittle from the lack of rain. If a fire came to this dry grass, it would burn more quickly than it would were the grass soft and sweet from normal, usual rains that fell this time of year.

As it was, danger lay all around him if a fire did begin.

He gazed heavenward.

The clouds continued to build, the sun hidden behind them.

Just one lightning strike, and everything could change so quickly. . . .

CHAPTER 2

I love thee freely, as men strive for Right.
I love thee purely, as they turn from Praise.
I love thee with the passion put to use
In my old griefs, and with my childhood's
faith.
— Elizabeth Barrett Browning

The clouds rolling across the heavens cast muted shadows on a mound of earth as Shiona Bramlett, age eighteen, stood beside the fresh grave of her father.

Her mother, Virginia, stood on Shiona's left side, and Seth, her younger brother by two years, stood on her right.

As Seth continued reading a verse from the family Bible, Shiona looked guardedly over her shoulder at the stagecoach that awaited her and her family.

Her father had been a colonel at Fort Chance; except for the few soldiers who remained to finalize things, the fort was abandoned as of this morning. Shiona, her mother, and her brother were the only remaining civilians at the site.

They had stayed behind long enough to say a final good-bye to their loved one and then would travel in the opposite direction from where the cavalry, and the others who lived with the cavalry, were headed.

Today, after they left the grave site, all three would board the stagecoach for the journey home to Kansas City, Missouri.

Shiona's gaze shifted to two horses that were tied to the rear of the stagecoach — steeds for herself and Seth.

After they got a short distance from Fort Chance, she and her brother planned to depart the stagecoach and mount their horses to search for their father's stash of gold.

After they found it, they planned to rejoin their mother on the long journey back to Missouri.

But they just couldn't leave without at least trying to find the map their father had hidden.

It had all begun when her father had returned from a long day away from the fort with the cavalry. They had been checking out the area to see if any Indians might be ready to cause trouble.

Her father had told the story of that day to his family in the privacy of their cabin. He said that he and those under his command had stopped to rest, but he had happened to go farther downstream for a drink.

As he had knelt and dipped his hands into the stream, he saw the shine of gold below on the rocky bed of the stream.

He had kept the knowledge of what he saw to himself, his mind spinning. How was he going to pan for the gold with no one else of the cavalry knowing?

By the time he had gotten back to the fort he had hatched a plan. He told his family that he planned to sneak away from the fort as often as possible. He would pan for the gold until he had enough to make it possible for him to leave the cavalry.

He and his family would then return to Kansas City and live the high life — they would have everything they ever wanted, and even more!

He also knew that he must do what he could quickly, because the fort was soon to be abandoned and he might lose his opportunity.

All of them, especially Shiona's mother, had pleaded with him not to do this, that it was too dangerous to be away from the fort alone, especially panning for gold.

But being the colonel in charge of the fort, he said that he could come and go as he pleased, and for them not to worry one iota about it. He was skilled with firearms. He could defend himself against any renegade or outsider who might come upon him alone.

It was then that he told them he had already begun his scheme without them or anyone else knowing. He had stored the gold he found in a drawstring bag in a cave.

The very afternoon after he had shared his amazing story, he hadn't arrived home. Everyone had become concerned, especially his family, who knew what he had been up to.

They all knew that something had to have happened to him. The cavalry had found him, not far from the fort, his horse grazing peacefully nearby.

An arrow was lodged in her father's back, but he was miraculously still alive . . . and he wanted to say good-bye to his family.

After he was returned to the fort, he had beckoned Shiona down closer to his lips. She was his favorite of his two children, and he told her to look in the family Bible. There she would find a map that would lead her to the cave where she would find a bag of gold and also another map that would lead to where he had found the gold.

He had encouraged Shiona to go with her brother and retrieve the gold and return with their mother to the safety of Missouri.

He told her to forget the map.

There was enough gold in the one bag to make them comfortable for the rest of their lives.

He had pleaded with her to do as he said, that the gold could give his wife the sort of life she never had because of his determination to stay in the military.

Her father had not lived long enough to tell them who had killed him, but all concluded it must have been an Indian, because an arrow was the weapon used to murder him.

Shiona shivered as she thought of the arrow that had been shown to her, which had been taken from her father's body. It was of a special design that she would never forget. . . .

Her thoughts were disturbed when she realized that she and her family were not alone. Besides the stagecoach driver and the man who rode as the gunman to protect them, she caught a glimpse of an Apache half-breed scout for the cavalry who stood nearby behind a tree watching and listening.

She could not help but wonder if that half-breed, whose name was Jack Thunder Horse, might somehow know about the gold.

Why else was he lurking so close by, his pale blue eyes taking in everything?

She knew that he had been assigned to stay behind with the few soldiers who were finalizing things at the fort.

But that had not included spying on Shiona and her family as they said private good-byes to their loved one!

She gave Jack Thunder Horse a glare, which made him turn and walk slowly away.

His long red hair, which contrasted strangely against his copper skin, worn in a braid down his back, was the last thing she saw as he disappeared amid the shadows of trees.

"Sis, it's time to go."

She turned and smiled softly at Seth. "Yes, I know," she murmured. "It's time to go."

Seth held their mother gently by an arm as he led her to the stagecoach, her golden hair now threaded with gray, only partially revealed beneath the bonnet she wore.

Shiona could not help but be concerned about her decision to leave her mother alone while she and her brother searched for the gold. The day she and Seth had explained the plan to her mother, she had grown faint, then had collected herself and said that she forbade it, that it was foolish, and that it was what had killed their father . . . fool's gold, that might be the downfall of his very own children.

They had tried hard to explain how the gold would make their lives so much easier, and that she deserved a nice home after having lived in small cabins, traveling from fort to fort as she followed her colonel husband.

Even then she argued, but neither Seth nor Shiona would take no for an answer, and the time had finally come for them to put their plan into action.

They boarded the stagecoach with their mother and rode for a while. At last the fort was far enough behind them, and Seth shouted up at the stagecoach driver to stop.

"Please don't do this," their mother pleaded, tears spilling from her eyes. "Son . . . Daughter . . . this could be a final good-bye. I just can't see how you can do what your father lost his life trying to do. Come on with me to Kansas City. Please, oh please, listen to your mother. Please listen to reason."

"Mama, we'll be all right," Shiona said,

placing a gentle hand on her mother's cheek. "We don't have that far to go to get to the cave. We'll grab the gold and join you again. Just think what sort of life you can lead, Mama, when we arrive in Kansas City. Please accept that we are planning to do this."

"Child, you are too headstrong," Virginia said. She grabbed one of Shiona's hands and then one of Seth's. She gazed from one to the other. "Please hurry," she said, a desperation in her eyes and voice.

"We shall," Shiona said, then gave her mother a long, warm hug.

Shiona watched Seth hug their mother, and then, after tying their travel bags securely to their horses, they rode away from the stagecoach, occasionally glancing over their shoulders at it, until it was out of their sight.

Then Shiona gazed up at the threatening clouds that were building overhead. "That's all we need now, Seth, a horrible storm," she said, then snapped her reins and sank her heels into the flanks of her steed, riding harder toward the direction of the cave.

"Sis, I hope we're doing the right thing," Seth said, drawing her eyes back to him. "I have a funny feeling. It's down deep in my gut. Maybe we should turn back and join

Mother after all."

"Seth, you are always having funny feelings about this and that. Little brother, you promised not to go scared on me," Shiona said. She frowned at him. "If we have anything to fear at all, it's those damnable clouds. It looks like it might pour at any moment."

She flinched when she saw a zigzag of lightning in the sky, then grimaced when a loud clap of thunder quickly followed.

"We've got to find the cave to keep from getting drenched," Shiona shouted over at him.

They rode onward over what was once soft and beautiful waving grass, but was now brittle beneath the hooves of the horses because of the lack of rain.

"We should be welcoming the rain, not dreading it," Seth said back to her. "When things are this dry, one spark from lightning could cause a terrible range fire."

"Seth, you're always looking on the sour side of life," Shiona said scoldingly. She sighed heavily. "Little brother, think positive this one time. Please?"

Suddenly it was not a roar of thunder that they heard.

It was a spattering of gunfire and screams behind them.

It came from the direction where they had left the stagecoach.

"Oh no. Oh, Lord, no!" Shiona cried as silence followed the screams.

"Shiona, do you think . . . ?" Seth said, his voice breaking.

"Seth, pray that it isn't what we both are thinking happened," Shiona said.

She wheeled her horse around and rode hard back in the direction of the stagecoach.

Seth was soon beside her, his face having grown pale from fear of what they might find.

"Shiona, maybe we'd better not go and see," Seth cried. "We'll surely be killed, too. You know that what we heard had to have been an attack on the stagecoach."

"Yes, and our mother might still be alive and needing us," Shiona said, not paying heed to her brother's warning.

Yet she realized that chances were she and her brother would be slaughtered if they returned now. She wheeled her horse to a quick stop.

"You're right," she said, wiping tears from her eyes as she gazed over at Seth. "If the stagecoach was ambushed, you know that no one was left . . . alive. We won't be any good to our mother now. We'll wait, Seth. We'll wait."

They went into hiding behind a thick stand of trees. When they couldn't stand the uncertainty any longer, they rode onward.

Both grew ill to their stomachs when they saw from a distance what had, indeed, happened.

The stagecoach had most certainly been attacked.

Both the driver and the man who sat guard beside him were on the ground next to the stopped stagecoach. They had been shot, and the horses were gone.

"I don't think I can stand looking inside the stagecoach," Seth said faintly. He reached a hand to his mouth to try and hold back the urge to vomit.

"If you don't want to look in the stagecoach, you don't have to," Shiona said over to him. "I shall, Seth, honey. I . . . shall."

"Thanks, Sis."

They arrived at the stagecoach. Shiona slid from the saddle, ran to the door, and slowly opened it. As she did, her mother's body tumbled to the ground, an arrow lodged in her belly.

Everything within Shiona went cold with grief. She fell to her knees and knelt over her mother, the arrow preventing her from being able to gather her mother into her arms as she so desperately wanted to do.

"Oh, Mama, what have they done to you?" she cried. "Mama. Oh, Mama!"

Seth fell to his knees beside them. "Mama was the only one killed by an arrow," he said, tears rushing from his eyes as he stared at his mother's blood-spattered dress.

"We must get her buried and get out of here as fast as we can," Shiona said, hating with every beat of her heart having to relinquish a second parent to the ground.

Seth trembled violently. "What . . . do . . . we do about the arrow?" he gulped out.

"Remove what we can," Shiona murmured.

"Lord, Shiona, I can't do it," Seth said, sobbing. "I . . . just . . . can't."

Having always been the stronger of the two of them, Shiona reached a comforting hand to his shoulder. "I'll do it, Seth," she said, her voice cracking with emotion. "Honey, I'll do it."

Sobbing, she finally managed to break the shaft, but couldn't help leaving a portion embedded in their mother's belly.

"What of the others?" Seth asked as he lifted his mother into his arms and began carrying her away from the massacre, stopping when they came to a stream, where the ground was not as hard as elsewhere.

"We can take the time only to bury

Mother, and then we've got to hightail it out of here," Shiona said, hardly able to see through her tears. She hurried back to the stagecoach and found a shovel on the top, then hurried back to Seth.

She and her brother soon had their mother in the ground, with words spoken over her. Then they carried the other two bodies down by the stream and covered them with rocks in order to keep them from being defiled by animals.

Grief-stricken, they hurried to their horses, only now truly realizing the danger they were in.

Would they, themselves, last one more day?

Were those who were responsible watching them even now, awaiting the right moment to kill them?

A loud clap of thunder interrupted their thoughts. "Seth, we must find that cave before the storm hits in its full fury," Shiona said, mounting her horse.

She gave her mother's grave one more long look, then wheeled her steed around, and with Seth beside her, rode again in the direction of the cave.

"How could this have happened?" Shiona cried, confused and heartsick.

Life would never, ever be the same again.

All that she had left in her life was her brother.

Lord have mercy were she to lose him, too!

CHAPTER 3

Ah! — With what thankless heart
I mourn and sing!

— Barry Cornwall

Still looking for his brother, Shadow Bear
clung hard to his horse's reins as his steed
steadily climbed a patch of steep terrain.
Finally he came to a place that leveled off,
where he could survey the land below him,
and pray that he would find his brother.

He drew a tight rein and stopped his stallion.

Surely the knowledge of where his brother
was would come to him, for this was a
sacred place, sheltered by the mountain.
This was the place where he had gained
magical powers.

A hawk had come to him here one fateful
day and shared its many secrets. And from
there on Shadow Bear had become as swift

as a hawk and feared nothing from any foe.

But today Shadow Bear was fearing something besides man. His foe today was the continued threat of the weather and the absence of his younger brother.

Since Shadow Bear had left his village, he had searched for the place his brother had taken the offering to the buffalo, but still had not found it. Now, from this vantage point, he could see far and wide. He scanned the land below him for any signs of Silent Arrow, still seeing nothing except . . .

His eyes widened and he leaned forward.

He clutched a hand to the pommel of his saddle to balance himself as he gazed in wonder at what he was seeing far down below him.

It was not his brother, but two other people, instead. Two strangers were coaxing their horses into a hard gallop through the parched grass.

One was a woman.

The other was a man.

Both had white skin.

But the woman was the one who drew his attention longer.

She had long and flowing golden hair, the wind lifting and fluttering it as she rode onward so determinedly.

Hoh! She was petite and beautiful, her

leather skirt hiked up above her knees, revealing boots that he did not know women wore.

He again gazed at her face.

He had truly never seen a woman as beautiful, not even among his own lovely Lakota women.

Realizing where his thoughts had taken him, and stunned that he could feel something for a woman with white skin, he turned his eyes quickly away from her.

He wanted nothing to do with any *washechu,* white eyes, except the one who had befriended him and his people. He was a Frenchman who made his home on land not that far from his people's village. His name was Pierre.

Besides this Frenchman, Shadow Bear and his people had had much trouble with whites since the white eyes had come to land that had from the beginning of time belonged solely to the Lakota!

He was avoiding the *washechus* now with every fiber of his being, for the less he and his people had to do with them, the less trouble erupted from such contact.

Before he turned away from those *washechus* who rode now below him, he studied the man who rode on his steed beside the woman. He could not help but want to know what this man was to her.

Was he her husband?

And if so, why would he allow his *tawicu,* wife, to ride so far from a white man's fort without the safety of armed escorts? He knew that Fort Chance should by now be totally abandoned, so might these two have come from there? Were they seeking a home elsewhere?

When *wakinyan-hoto,* lightning, suddenly gave birth to sound, thunder, as lurid streaks brightened up what had become a day almost turned night by darkening clouds, Shadow Bear's attention was drawn from the interlopers on Lakota land.

He winced when the ensuing clap of thunder echoed all around him and shook the hard rocky ground beneath him. He looked quickly overhead.

On clear days the sky was as blue as Lakota-blue paint. But today it was as though a being in the heavens had wiped it clean of such a lustrous blue color and exchanged it for an ominous black, as the clouds grew in intensity.

Ho, yes, the thunderers were building more and more dark clouds.

It was a world of clouds.

A thunderstorm was definitely imminent, coming now from where the sun went down. The dark clouds were now piled like mountains across the sky and in them thunder beings lived and leaped and flashed.

His grandmother's vision of a great *peta,* fire, came to his mind. It would surely come from a lightning strike on dry grass, for thus far, no rain fell from the heavens, only lightning.

He knew he must be on his way. He had hoped to find his brother before the fire began, but now he doubted that would be so.

Remembering the woman and man, he realized they could be in danger of the fire's fury, too. But during his moments of studying the sky they had ridden onward and were now out of sight.

Realizing they surely were in danger of being trapped by the flames of the fire of his grandmother's vision, Shadow Bear was torn with what he should do.

A part of him wanted to search them out and warn them, because he could not imagine that beautiful, petite woman being caught amid the ugly, raging flames that would soon overtake the land.

But his brother was his sole purpose for being this far from his home. So he put the woman from his mind, his brother again his main concern. He must find him soon, or perhaps never see him again.

But first, above all else, before leaving the mountain to search elsewhere, he needed the solace of prayer. Again he looked heavenward. "Oh, *Wakan-Tanka,* grandfather of us all, give me power to see far beyond this place. Give me knowledge to find my brother. Give me the strength and swiftness again of the hawk so that I can find my brother!"

Feeling the blessing of *Wakan-Takan,* and eager now to be on his way, Shadow Bear rode away from this high place of prayer.

When he was down on level ground again, he kneed his steed and rode in a hard gallop across the land. His long black hair flying in the wind, he sought out places where he still might find his brother, yet his mind strayed more often than not to the golden-haired woman.

He could not help but search for her, too, as he tried hard to find his brother before the foretold fires began, for he still could not imagine this woman dying by the hungry fingers of that fire!

CHAPTER 4

Go from me. Yet I feel that I shall stand
Henceforward in thy shadow.
> — Elizabeth Barrett Browning

"I see it!" Shiona shouted through the loud rumbling of thunder. "Seth. The cave. It's over there." She pointed to it. "Do you see it, too?"

"It's about time," Seth said, nodding. He gazed heavenward and cringed when he saw the worsening display of flashes of fury in the sky.

"I don't like this lightning," he cried. "We've got to get inside the cave. While we're out here in the open, we could be a target of a lightning strike."

"Yes, I know," Shiona said. She sank her heels into the flanks of her horse and sent it into a harder gallop toward the cave entrance.

Once there, they tied their horses' reins to a low tree limb, hurriedly gathered as much firewood as they could, and ran with it inside the cave.

"Let's get away from the entrance so that when the rain starts it doesn't blow in on us," Shiona said. She found it hard to believe that they were actually in the cave where her father had hidden the map and his sack of gold. But for now she and her brother had more important things to do. They worked together at getting the fire started, then took the time to look around them as the fire's glow spread on all three sides of the cave and beyond.

Shiona choked up a bit as she could almost feel her father's presence in the cave with them. "I miss him so," she blurted out. She wiped tears from her eyes. "I wish Father had never seen that gold in the stream. If he hadn't, we'd all still be a family. But as it is, Mother is also now gone from us."

Seth went to her and pulled her into his gentle embrace. "Now it's only us, Sis," he said, his voice thick with emotion. "And although I am younger, I will protect you."

"I know," Shiona said, clinging, although she knew about his shyness and delicate sensibilities. She had to accept that she was now in charge of not only her own destiny, but also her baby brother's.

She flinched and turned away from Seth when another clap of thunder echoed into the cave, bouncing from wall to wall in an almost deafening pounding. "We've got to get the horses inside and out of the weather," she said, hurrying toward the cave entrance. She looked over her shoulder at her brother. "And, Seth, I'm hungry. As we came into the cave I saw some grapevines twining through the bushes. The grapes were the fattest I have ever seen. I'll pick some as you secure our horses."

While Seth got the horses and led them far back into the cave, Shiona gathered together several grapes and took them back inside, joining Seth.

"Spread the blankets and we shall have a feast of grapes as we sit and rest before heading out again after we find the gold," Shiona said, watching her brother spread a blanket beside the fire.

She looked over her shoulder in the direction of the horses, then sat down with Seth on the blanket and began eating the nourishing grapes.

"Will the horses be all right back there in the darkness?" Shiona asked, again looking in their direction.

Seth nodded, swallowing bites of the sweet grapes. "The fire's glow reaches as far back as where they are tethered, and there is a small stream from which they can drink."

"Seth, did you taste the water to see if it is pure and clean enough for the horses?" Shiona asked. "It could be heavy with minerals that would poison them and make them deathly ill."

"No, I didn't think of testing it," Seth said, sighing. He nodded toward the steeds. "Maybe you should go and take a taste, Sis. Or do you want me to?"

"I'll do it," Shiona said, moving quickly to her feet. "You sit there and rest. We've got a lot ahead of us."

"You should be the one to rest, not me," Seth said. He smiled up at her as she started walking toward the back of the cave. "You're the lady, Sis."

"And when has that ever mattered between us when it came time for us to do this or that?" Shiona said laughingly as she gazed affectionately at her brother. "I won't be long. Eat the rest of the grapes. There are many more where they came from."

Seth nodded and plopped another grape in his mouth as Shiona walked toward the horses.

When she reached them, she saw the tiny

44

stream as it seeped in between cracks along the side wall of the cave. She took the time to pat both horses, then bent to her knees and brought some of the water into her mouth. After getting a good taste, she concluded that it was as fresh as anything she would find outside, so she pushed herself up from the cave floor and took the time to hug each horse.

"We won't be in here for long, sweet things," she murmured as she gave her own personal steed another hug, then stroked his neck. "Once the storm passes over I'll take you both back outside."

Her steed whinnied and leaned its nose into her hand and nuzzled it, then contented itself again by taking another drink of the water.

Seeing that things were all right with the horses, Shiona walked quickly toward the glow of the fire. She stopped abruptly when she saw that Seth was gone.

"I guess he went for more firewood before it rains," Shiona said, then giggled. "Or he went for more fat grapes."

She sat down on the blanket again, her eyes moving slowly along the wall of the cave. After she and Seth rested, they would search for the small sack of gold.

It wouldn't hurt to wait. It was there with

them in the cave. It was most certainly not going anywhere.

Feeling suddenly chilled, Shiona reached for another blanket and swept it around her shoulders.

She flinched when she heard another great clap of thunder, closer this time, the lightning reflecting into the mouth of the cave.

She looked toward the cave entrance and saw how everything outside was so much darker now as the clouds loomed lower over the land.

Something grabbed at her heart and she screamed when Seth stumbled into the cave and then fell to the floor onto his back.

The fire's glow, and another lurid flash of lightning, revealed an arrow in her brother's chest as he lay there, wildly clawing at it.

With a quick glance, Shiona noted that it was an arrow with two red wavering lines along each side, the same sort of arrow that had killed not only her father, but also her mother.

"Oh, Seth!" Shiona cried as she leaped to her feet and rushed to him.

"Sis, do something . . . ," Seth cried, his eyes wild, tears flooding them.

"Oh, Seth, this time I don't think there is anything I can do for you," Shiona cried as she fell to her knees beside him. She ached to pull him into her arms, to cradle him, because she knew that he was dying.

But she couldn't.

Just as with her mother, the damnable arrow was in the way!

As she sat there, staring disbelievingly at her dying brother, her sobs echoed ominously back at her on all sides as they bounced off one wall and then another.

She screamed again when a louder, closer clap of thunder rumbled immediately after she saw a great, huge bolt of lightning hitting something not that far from the cave, sparks flying.

She gasped when she saw a fire beginning and quickly spreading through the parched grass, no rain yet to fall to hinder the fire's progress.

She looked at Seth. She felt as though her heart were tearing apart when she saw that his eyes were locked in a death stare. She could hardly believe it, yet she knew that it was true. She had now also lost her brother!

Sobbing, she gently closed his eyes. "Seth, I wish I could've helped," she cried, reaching out now and gently touching his cheek. She soaked up his tears with the flesh of her fingers, then looked quickly away from him and closed her eyes.

She had never felt as helpless as now.

In truth, she was alone in this horrible world!

Knowing that her fate rested in her own hands, Shiona quickly collected herself. She had another member of her family who required burying.

"But where?" she cried, still holding Seth endearingly to her bosom, slowly rocking him lovingly back and forth.

"Seth. Oh, Seth, tell me what to do," she sobbed, as she looked at his closed eyes and then at the hideousness of the arrow as it still stuck from his chest.

"I must remove that thing before I do anything else," she whispered. Just as she had done for her mother, she would do the same for her brother.

Resigned to her task, she broke the shaft of the arrow in half. As with her mother, a portion of that arrow was still lodged in her brother's chest.

"It will be with you for eternity," she whispered, gently smoothing some of his golden hair back from his brow.

The knowledge that she was alone in the world made nausea grab at the pit of her belly.

"I must get ahold of myself," she said aloud, her chin firm, her jaw tight. "I now have only myself and must see to my own

48

destiny. And . . . and . . . I shall make it. I'm strong. Nothing is going to defeat me now."

Except . . .

She paled when she thought of how her brother had died.

By an arrow.

And an arrow had to be shot from a bowstring!

And a bow had to be handled by someone who shot the arrow from the string!

"Lord almighty, I'm surely next," she said, trembling.

But the smell of smoke coming from the outside where the fire was spreading in leaps and bounds miraculously made hope rise within her.

The storm might have run off the assailant who had killed her brother. He would need to escape the flames of the fire.

She hoped that she was right, and that she might have more time now to do what she must for her brother.

She gently grabbed him beneath his arms and started dragging him toward the back of the cave, past the horses, where the campfire's glow now barely reached.

Shiona reached around on the floor of the cave.

She discovered that the rocks there were

49

only thinly strewn, and beneath it was soft earth.

This would work for her brother's grave.

She hurried back to her supplies and removed a pickax that was meant to be used for looking for gold.

Instead, it would help her dig a grave.

As she began digging into the earthen floor, after moving the rocks away, she kept a cautious eye on the cave's entrance. She knew that a murderer could not be too far away. Surely it was the same person, an Indian no less, who killed her father, mother, and now her brother.

"Yes, it has to be the same person," Shiona whispered to herself. The same identical design of the arrows was proof.

If she made it out of this thing alive, she knew what to look for. If she ever saw anyone with this same design on an arrow in their possession, she would have found the murderer.

She struggled, but finally got her beloved brother buried.

She scattered rock as thickly as she could atop the grave, to keep four-legged predators from coming and defiling his body once she was gone.

She said a prayer over the grave, placed a hand lovingly on the mound of dirt and rock, then went back to the campfire.

As she sat there, staring at one half of the arrow that had penetrated her brother's body, she reached for it and angrily tossed it into the flames of the fire. Then she stared at the blood on the floor of the cave, where her brother had lain.

She stood up, kicked loose rock over the blood until she couldn't see it any longer, then fell back down onto the spread blanket and held her face in her hands, sobbing.

When the first rush of grief had passed and she was able to think clearly, she realized that she must take precautions. She grabbed her rifle and rested it on her lap.

She hoped the fire had made the murderer give up for today. But what about tomorrow, and all tomorrows that lay ahead of her? Shiona could not help but wonder.

"I do know one thing, I'll be ready for you, you coward," she said with a vengeance in her voice that surprised her.

She had always been a gentle soul, filled with love and peace.

But now?

All bets were off.

A murderer had changed everything.

"Especially me," she said in a low growl.

CHAPTER 5

. . . Doom takes to part us, leaves thy
    heart in mine,
With pulses that beat double.
                    — Elizabeth Barrett Browning

The raging fire had sent Shadow Bear riding hard toward his village, and when he arrived he was glad to see that his people had prepared well for the fire.

As he had instructed his warriors to do, the trenches had been dug on the two sides of the village. They were wide and deep enough to keep back the flames that could destroy his people's lives.

In at least that, they had been successful. Otherwise, he had come home empty-handed after having again failed to find any signs of his brother.

Ho, yes, it was as though Silent Arrow had disappeared from the face of the earth, and

52

Shadow Bear could not understand why.

Shadow Bear rode on to his tepee, dismounted, then handed his reins over to Two Leaves, a young brave who was assigned to care for his chief's steeds in all respects.

He gazed slowly toward his grandmother's tepee. She must have heard his horse upon his arrival to the village, for she was standing in the doorway of her lodge.

She gazed back at Shadow Bear with tears streaming down her tautly drawn skin. *Ho,* yes, she knew without even asking that Shadow Bear had not been successful at finding Silent Arrow.

Shadow Bear walked sullenly to his grandmother.

He took her by an elbow and slowly walked her into her tepee, then once there, turned her to face him.

"There were no signs of Silent Arrow anywhere," he said thickly. He reached his hands to her face and smoothed tears from her cheeks with the flesh of his thumbs.

"Grandmother," he then said, "being the astute person that he is, Silent Arrow surely saw the danger of the storm, as we saw it, and sought shelter. He surely thought that he could not return home quickly enough to escape the fire."

"But, *Mitakoza,* Grandson, like you, Silent

53

Arrow has a fast, trusting horse," Dancing Breeze said, searching Shadow Bear's eyes. "You have come and gone from our village already in the time that your brother has been gone. He surely would have made it home, as well, unless . . ."

"*Ho,* yes, I know," Shadow Bear said, gently drawing her into his arms.

He hugged her to him, his heart aching anew when once again he was reminded of just how much his grandmother had wasted away to almost all bone since her mourning began for her husband and son, Shadow Bear's and Silent Arrow's *ahte,* father.

He could feel the sharpness of her bones through her clothes as she pressed herself against him to gather strength and courage from him.

Then he placed his hands at her waist and gently held her away from him so that they could look again into each other's eyes.

"Grandmother, while I was gone, did you, perhaps, see another vision?" he asked. "Did you see Silent Arrow?"

"No, no other vision came to me, as I prayed that it would," Dancing Breeze murmured. "Perhaps I have prayed too hard?"

"One can never pray too hard," Shadow Bear said emphatically. "Prayer is what

54

makes one have courage when, otherwise, the person can be filled with such despair they no longer want to live. Grandmother, you never want to get that lost in your mourning, or your despair of the moment. Without you, my world would be so empty. You are my world, Grandmother. You are all of our people's world. They depend on your visions. They love you, as well, just for yourself and the person you have always been. So, Grandmother, please do not get lost any further in worries and mourning, or I might be the one who is made to mourn for you."

"My dear chieftain *mitakoza,* grandson, I do not wish to bring such pain inside your heart, nor concern," Dancing Breeze said. She placed a gentle hand to his cheek. "You have responsibilities as chief that lay heavy on your shoulders. I want to help lighten your burdens, not make them heavier."

Shadow Bear swept her into his arms again. "Grandmother, Grandmother, all will be well," he said thickly. "You shall see. In time, all will be well. Once the fire is past and my brother can find his way back home again, we will both see how foolish it was of us to doubt his ability to take care of himself."

"*Ho,* yes, I know," Dancing Breeze said.

She stepped away from him and went and sat down on blankets before her fire pit, where no fire burned because of this day being so hot and uncomfortable.

She gazed up at Shadow Bear. "You go now and tend to your chieftain duties while I pray some more about Silent Arrow," she said, her voice drawn. "Perhaps during this time of prayer a vision will come to me and tell me where your brother is, and if he is well . . . or . . . dead."

Shadow Bear stepped up to her and placed a gentle, reassuring hand on her shoulder, then stepped outside her lodge.

He gazed heavenward.

Storm warriors continued to throw their lightning sticks to the earth, shaking the ground with their thunder. Yet the rain still did not fall from the sky.

CHAPTER 6

I strove to hate, but vainly strove.
— George Lyttelton

Daybreak sent splashes of light into the cave, awakening Shiona. She groaned as nausea swept through her. "Lordy, lordy," she whispered as she tried to sit up, but fell back down on the blankets from dizziness.

She placed a hand on her stomach when cramps grabbed at her insides. She moaned, knowing that she would feel better if she could vomit, but she couldn't. Whatever was causing her to feel so ill seemed to just lie there in her belly, twisting and turning.

She realized now that she was also becoming feverish. She reached a hand to her brow, wincing when she felt the heat against the flesh of her fingers.

It stunned her that she was ill.

While growing up, she had rarely been

sick. "As strong as an ox," her father had always said about her, even though she had always been such a tiny thing.

"What caused this?" she whispered, again trying to sit up, this time achieving it.

As she trembled from the rising fever, she grabbed her blanket up from the floor of the cave and swept it around her shoulders. She tried to think through things that she had done these past days, wondering what could have made her so ill. The main trauma she had experienced was the loss of her family.

Tears filled her eyes as she gazed toward the back of the cave, where her brother lay beneath a mound of dirt and rocks. "Oh, Seth, how can any of this truly be happening?" she cried. "I miss you so much. I . . . am . . . so alone. And now I am sick. Seth. Oh, Seth, I need you."

She hung her head in her hands as sobs racked her body, but then they suddenly stopped when she remembered something else.

The horses.

They were at the back of the cave.

The water.

She had left them by the tiny stream for them to be able to have nourishing water until she could take them back outside, where she would hopefully find some grass that had not burned.

She had also drunk from that stream.

Yes, surely the water had poisoned her.

She recalled a creek outside, not that far from the cave. She must take the horses there.

Knowing that she had to care for the horses, especially if they were also ill, Shiona managed to get to her feet, and although dizzy from the fever, she reached the back of the cave where the horses did seem somewhat ill.

Shiona glanced at her brother's grave, stopped long enough to say a soft prayer, then took the horses' reins and walked them slowly through the cave, until they finally reached the entrance, went outside, and stepped into wet ash.

It was only then that Shiona realized rain had surely fallen through the night, for everything was wet.

When she reached the creek, she dropped the reins and fell to her knees to taste the water.

After discovering it clean and fresh to the taste, she stood and shakily led her horses over to the water. On the embankment, where the fires had not reached, lay a soft stretch of grass, which would feed the horses.

She secured the reins, then watched one steed drink from the creek, while the other eagerly munched on the grass.

"You are going to be all right," she murmured, but she was not so sure about herself.

She turned and staggered toward the cave, where she knew she must sleep some more.

Surely she would get past this illness soon enough, and then she had to figure out what to do with the rest of her life, for she was going to have to live it alone.

But for now, all she wanted was sleep.

Her eyelids were heavy with the need of it.

Her body was almost limp with the fever now.

She couldn't remember ever having such a temperature, not even when she came down with the measles when she was seven years of age.

Seth had gotten the measles at the same time and they had shared a bedroom, each in their own bed, their mother sweetly taking care of them.

But Shiona never wanted another bowl of tomato soup for the rest of her life, for that was all that her mother had fed them until the spots on their bodies began to fade along with their fevers.

Fear grabbed at her heart and she stopped with a start when she saw an Indian dressed in only a breechclout and moccasins step into view a few feet away, just in front of the cave entrance. They had momentary eye contact, and then he collapsed.

It was then that Shiona came out of her fretful trance and saw the same sort of arrow that had downed her loved ones lodged in the Indian's shoulder. For a moment she wasn't sure what she should do, but she did know one thing: She was in the company of an Indian and he was injured enough to have now passed out.

She still stood there, staring back at him.

Surely an Indian had killed her loved ones, so shouldn't she just leave this Indian be, to die as her loved ones had died?

But again she gazed at the arrow that had downed this Indian.

It was the sort that had downed her family.

That had to mean that this Indian was innocent.

Drawing upon her courage and strength she crept up to him and knelt beside him.

The blood from his wound had run down his arm and splashed over onto his bare, muscled chest. She knew that something had to be done about his wound or he would die!

But still, he was an Indian. She had been taught to stay away from and to fear all Indians, because they resented the white race. Yet her compassionate side would not allow her to leave the man be.

But the nausea that still swept through her, as well as her weakened state caused by the fever, made her realize that she would be lucky to care for herself these next few days while she fought off the fever, much less take care of an injured Indian.

She flinched with a start when his eyes suddenly opened and one of his hands reached out for her.

"Help me," he said in perfect English.

Shiona was stunned by this Indian's use of English.

But she remembered now how her father had told her that most redskins in this area were able to speak the English language. They had learned it from priests who came and went in hopes of civilizing the red man with the white man's religion. Also, knowing the white man's language helped the Indians during their times of trade with whites.

"Who shot you?" she finally asked. She

fought hard to keep her senses with the fever attacking her brain.

"An . . . unseen . . . assailant," he said, his midnight-dark eyes still pleading with her. "The assailant shot me . . . and . . . left me for dead."

He looked more intently into her eyes. "You are ill," he said, having noted her flushed, fevered countenance. "Are . . . you . . . strong enough to . . . help me into the cave? Both you and I will be safer there."

Shiona was torn with what to do. Once they were inside the cave, could he muster up enough strength to kill her?

Yet there was such a gentleness about him and in his eyes that she truly doubted he would hurt her, even if he were strong and well enough to do it.

And he did need her help. The arrow had caused much damage in his shoulder and he had lost quite a bit of blood.

No. She just could not ignore anyone who was in need of help, not even an Indian.

Mustering her strength, Shiona managed to get him inside the cave beside what was left of the fire. She reached over and got her canteen of water. Then she opened it and held it to his lips, watching him as he gulped it down in great, deep swallows.

When he was finished, he gently shoved it

away. "Enough," he said weakly. "Save some for yourself."

Seeing the kind side of this Indian, Shiona smiled. She now had more trust in him and what she was doing.

She screwed the lid back on the canteen, then again gazed at his wound and the portion of the arrow that protuded from his shoulder.

She knew that the arrow must be removed, but how?

She knew nothing about such things.

"The arrow," she gulped out. "It should be removed. But I don't know about such things as that."

She was again fighting back a nausea that kept her belly feeling as though something were inside it, clawing at it. But she had someone else to think about besides herself.

She did know the danger of that arrow remaining in the Indian's flesh. It could poison him. He could die.

"I will instruct you if you are strong enough to remove it," the Indian said, searching her eyes. "It is necessary to remove the arrow, for if I am to live, the arrow must be taken out and my wound medicated."

"I'm afraid to remove it," Shiona said, her

64

voice breaking. "What if you bleed to death?"

"I have medicine that will keep that from happening," the Indian said, reaching for a small buckskin bag from the waistband of his breechclout.

He looked into her eyes again. "What is your name?" he asked, holding the bag out for her to take.

"Shiona," she shyly told him.

"I am called by the name Silent Arrow," he said, smiling through his pain.

Shiona took the bag and gazed down at it.

"Open it," Silent Arrow urged, stretching out on his back, the weakness claiming him more by the minute. He knew the urgency and importance of getting medicated quickly, or he might not make it back to his home alive.

Shiona nodded and did as he said.

Inside were some strange-looking roots and some sort of berries. She questioned him with her eyes.

"I gathered these things before the fire began, to use once I found someone to remove the arrow," Silent Arrow said, his voice weakening. "If I had not found you today, I most likely would have died."

"How did you survive the fire?" Shiona asked.

"By finding a high, dry place until the rains came and extinguished the fire all around me," Silent Arrow explained. "That place was just above us, the ground that covered the cave. It was from that high place that I saw you leave with the horses. It was then that I came down to ask your help. It is good that you do not see me as an enemy as most whites would, and that you are willing to help me even though I know that you are quite ill yourself."

Shiona's eyes widened. "How do you know that?" she gasped.

"I know a face that is hot with fever, for it happens too often to my own people," Silent Arrow said softly.

"Yes, I am ill, perhaps too ill to help you do what you are asking of me," Shiona said. "I . . . I . . . don't have a steady enough hand for which to do this."

"You must or I will surely die," Silent Arrow said. "You might die, too, if you do not take the medicine I offer you for your fever."

Shiona winced and fear grabbed at her heart when Silent Arrow suddenly slid his knife from the sheath at his right side.

But she quickly knew that she was wrong to have been afraid when he gently handed it to her.

"Take the knife," he said thickly. "Hold it

into the heat that remains of your fire, but first eat the juniper berries that you will find in the bag. I will eat some, too, for I am now feeling feverish from my wound. Take a deep swallow of water after eating the berries."

She did as he told her while he ate his own berries; then they shared the water from the canteen.

This was all so surreal to Shiona.

Oh, surely she was dreaming it!

She had never had any sort of connection with Indians before. She had been taught to be wary of them at all times.

"Shiona, hold the knife into the heat of the fire," Silent Arrow again urged, trust in his eyes as she took the knife in her hand. "As you hold the knife into the heat, I will prepare the other medicine that you will use on my wound once the arrow is removed. Hand me the bag."

Trembling, and still so nauseous and feverish that she could hardly kneel there, Shiona did as he asked while he explained what medicine he was preparing for her to use on his wound. He had found a purple cone plant, which was a single-stalked plant called the *ica-hpe-hu,* which was a long, slender black root.

"After the arrow is removed, you are to

chew this plant and apply it to my injury," he said. "It will not only ease my pain, but will in time cure my wound."

She broke the arrow shaft.

Grimacing, she slid the one half from the wound, then proceeded to cut the other half from his body. After she placed the medicine on his wound, she collapsed.

She fell into a drugged sort of sleep as Silent Arrow gazed at her, then rose shakily to his feet.

He started to leave, but chose to first add wood to the fire so that the heat from it would help her as she trembled with chills.

He took one long look at her, then turned and quietly left the cave.

He managed to get to the horses that he had seen her lead to the water. His own had been frightened away by the lightning.

He took one of the steeds and managed to get on it, bareback, then rode away.

He knew that the woman with the fascinating name Shiona would be all right because he had given her the medicine that would make her well.

That was all that mattered.

And it was only right that he had seen to her welfare before going on home to his people. She had given of herself to him, so had he given of himself to her.

CHAPTER 7

The pure and perfect moment briefly
  caught
As in your arms, but still a child, I lay.
                — Vita Sackville-West

Shadow Bear was awakened by his grand-mother's voice outside of his tepee. He gazed up and through the smoke hole and saw a perfectly blue sky. He remembered how it had finally rained through the night, extinguishing the flames that had devastated the land beyond his village.

There had been a few exceptions. Some flying debris from the nearby fire had breached the deep trench that had been dug, setting fire to two tepees, which had quickly been put out by several warriors who threw water onto the flames.

"Shadow Bear?"

His grandmother's voice spoke again just

beyond his closed entrance flap.

Not wanting to keep her waiting, he threw aside his blanket and slid into a breechclout and moccasins.

While flipping his long, sleek hair so that it hung down his back, he went to the entrance flap and untied it, then hurriedly swept it aside.

"Come inside, Grandmother," Shadow Bear said. He took her gently by an elbow and helped her through the doorway.

"Why have you come so early to speak with me?" he asked as he helped ease her down on blankets opposite the fire pit. He only now realized the coolness of the day, the rain having eased the heat spell they had been living through.

He noticed how his grandmother clung to the shawl she had around her bent shoulders, and saw the purplish hew to her lips. He knew that she was uncomfortably chilled, and began to build a fire while she explained why she had come.

"You have had another vision?" Shadow Bear asked, settling down opposite the fire from his grandmother. "And you said that Silent Arrow was not a part of the vision. So what did you see this time, Grandmother, that was compelling enough to bring you to my lodge this early morning?"

"In my vision was a golden-haired white lady, a petite woman who . . . ," Dancing Breeze began, trailing off in midsentence when she saw her grandson's reaction.

"You dreamed of a white woman and her hair was golden?" Shadow Bear asked, blushing.

The woman he'd seen during his search for his brother was the loveliest woman he had ever seen, and so petite he felt that a slight wind might even lift her from the saddle on which she rode.

He remembered something else, too.

She was carrying a rifle in a gun boot at the side of her steed, something else he was not used to seeing when he gazed upon women, both white and red-skinned.

"*Mitakoza,* Grandson, I see it in your eyes that you are seeing this woman that I spoke of, but not as a vision, but something quite real inside your mind and heart," Dancing Breeze said.

She again searched Shadow Bear's eyes, to seek answers.

"Grandson, do you know of such a woman?" Dancing Breeze asked softly.

"*Ho,* yes, I have seen a woman of your description," Shadow Bear replied. "Yesterday, before the fire interrupted all of our lives, I saw the white woman and the man

71

she rode side by side with."

He leaned forward somewhat. "But what is strange to me is that you saw her in your vision, yet had surely not ever seen her otherwise," he said, himself now searching his grandmother's eyes. "Why is that, Grandmother? How can that be?"

"Why I see visions, and who I see in them, is not only a mystery to you, but also myself," Dancing Breeze said, slowly smiling, causing her eyes to seem to dance with a quiet, yet proud, amusement.

Then her smile waned. "I must tell you more about my vision and the woman that I saw in it," she said softly. "The golden-haired lady was ill."

"Ill?" Shadow Bear said, finding it strange how hearing this made his heart momentarily skip a beat. "In what way was she ill, and is it the sort of illness that might take . . . her . . . life?"

"I believe she will be well soon," Dancing Breeze murmured. "You see, I saw someone else in my vision."

"Who else?" he said, expecting her to mention the white man that he had seen with the white woman, surprised when he heard what she had truly seen.

"Myself," Dancing Breeze said matter-of-factly. "I saw myself with her."

"You?" Shadow Bear said, forking an eyebrow. "You saw yourself? In what respect?"

"I was in a cave, sitting beside the ill woman," Dancing Breeze said, smiling. "I spoke softly to her as I cared for her, bathing her feverish brow with fresh, cold water, applied to her skin with a soft piece of doeskin. I even sang to her in my vision. And then when I saw that her fever had lessened and she seemed so much better, I returned home and that is when I awakened with the vision so real to me I truly felt that I had been there with, and for, the white woman."

Amazed by what his grandmother had just told him, Shadow Bear was momentarily rendered speechless.

"I must return now to my own lodge and prepare myself with prayers for the day ahead of me," Dancing Breeze said. She slowly pushed herself up from the blanketed floor. "But something brought me here to you, to share my vision with you, even though it had nothing to do with your missing brother," Dancing Breeze then said. "This woman. Surely she exists. She is alone in the world, for there was no one with her in my vision but myself. You might want to search for her and offer her guidance. It was in a cave that I saw her. I am certain that if you search for that cave, you will find the woman."

Shadow Bear stood quickly and went to his grandmother. He embraced her before she stepped from the lodge.

"While I search for my brother, I will also search for the woman," he said gravely. "I know of such a cave. I shall see if she is there."

"Oh, my *mitakoza*, grandson, please bring Silent Arrow home to me," Dancing Breeze suddenly sobbed, her thin arms reaching around him, hugging him endearingly. "I fear so much for his safety. He . . . has . . . been gone for too long and he might have gotten caught amid the flames."

"I shall go and search again while you pray that my search will be successful," Shadow Bear said. "I will not even take the time to eat, for food will await my return. Pray for Silent Arrow and for my successful search."

"It will be so," Dancing Breeze said softly, then stepped away from Shadow Bear, leaving him alone with his thoughts.

"Why would my grandmother see this woman in her vision?" he whispered to himself as he placed his sheathed knife at his waist.

He stopped long enough to run his long,

lean fingers through his hair, then slid a headband in place so that his hair would not trouble him as he rode hard on his steed.

"What could be the connection to the white woman and my Lakota people?" he then asked as he grabbed his rifle. "My grandmother's visions always have a reason for having been brought to her. Why the white woman? Why not Silent Arrow?"

With effort, he pushed the woman from his mind and walked toward the corral. He chose his favored steed, Star, and saddled him. He mounted, then paused long enough to see where the trenches had all been filled up again, the danger of the fire behind his people.

He looked as far as the eye could see, where the fire had swept over the land beyond his village. Everywhere he looked things were black with ash. There was no sign of life.

The animals that had not been caught amid the flames had successfully fled in front of the heat and smoke and had not returned. Possibly they never would.

He saw no buffalo in the distance as he did some early mornings.

He did not see or hear birds.

And what saddened him to the very core of himself was how the fields of sunflowers lay dead on the scorched earth, their stalks and flowers turned now to ash.

And, oh, how the Lakota loved pure water, pure air, and a clean place for hunting, all of which were tainted by the fire and the continued smell of ash.

He heard his people stirring in their homes, and saw some women already on their way to the river for water. Reminded of how quickly the day was advancing, he knew that he should not wait any longer before heading out again to search for his brother.

"And the woman," he whispered to himself as he sank his moccasined heels into the flanks of his horse and rode off at a hard gallop toward a cave he knew of. He would check and see if the woman was there, and on his way, he would continue to search for any signs of his brother.

CHAPTER 8

My steps are nightly driven
By the fever in my breast
To hear from thy lattice breathed
The word that shall give me rest.

— Bayard Taylor

Shiona was halfway between sleep and waking, in her mind a vague, yet real remembrance of a dream that she'd had during the night. An elderly Indian woman had come to her, speaking softly to her. The elderly woman had also bathed Shiona's brow with water as she softly sang an Indian song to her.

And then the woman was gone as quickly as she had come.

Her eyes slowly opened, wishing the dream were real and that the woman was still there.

But when Shiona finally opened her eyes,

she gasped, then screamed. There were large spiders on the walls and ceiling of the cave, crawling lazily around. Suddenly one of the spiders lost its footing and began falling toward Shiona. She screamed again, over and over, her cries echoing eerily in the cave.

She sat up quickly and looked around her. But no spiders were there. So glad that it had been only a hallucination and not real, she cried with relief as she fell back down on the blanket, trembling. The fever was causing her to hallucinate.

Surely then the dream that she had had of the elderly woman was only that . . . a dream.

She was chilled through and through with the coolness of the cave.

"Mama," she whispered, needing her mother now more than ever before in her life. She drew a blanket more snugly and warmly around her. "Please, oh please, Mama, come . . . back . . . to me . . . ," she softly pleaded.

With only her memories to sustain her, Shiona closed her eyes and fell into another troubled sleep, not realizing that she was not alone after all. Shadow Bear had heard the screams as he had approached the cave.

Everything was quiet now.

The screams had stopped.

Shadow Bear hurriedly dismounted and tied his reins to a low limb of a tree, ignoring the lone horse that stood a short distance from the cave, munching on a small patch of green grass that the fire had not reached.

He hurried inside the cave, then stopped when he saw the woman huddled beneath a blanket beside a campfire that had almost burned out from neglect.

He went to the woman and knelt down beside her.

He was not at all stunned to see that it was the woman he had seen the previous day, riding with the man. He had, deep down inside himself, hoped that he would see her again, for everything about her had fascinated him.

Her loveliness.

Her skill at riding a horse.

Her long and beautiful hair, the color of summer wheat, fluttering in the air behind her as she sent her horse into a faster gallop.

But he also remembered how whites despised people with red skin, so he was afraid to awaken her, afraid that seeing him might frighten her.

Seeing how she was trembling, he realized that, true to his grandmother's vision, she was suffering from fever and the effects of the damp cave.

He hurriedly placed some logs in the fire pit. Then he bent low and blew on the embers beneath the logs, stirring up enough of them to send flames wrapping around the logs.

Feeling the warmth himself, even welcoming it since all that he wore today was a breechclout and moccasins, he rubbed his hands over the fire, then focused his full attention once again on the woman.

His heart pounding, he could not help but touch her beautiful face. As his flesh touched hers, he discovered that her face was so soft . . . yet so hot.

As she slowly began opening her eyes, he yanked his hand away from her. The fire's glow showed him that her eyes were the color of the violets that grew rampant along the forest floor in the spring.

He was surprised when she did not cry out with fear, or try to back away from him. Instead of fear when she realized that she was not alone, he saw some sort of relief when she gazed at him.

But he was taken fully aback when she tried to reach a hand out to him while softly speaking the name Silent Arrow.

She had just spoken his brother's name!

Why?

How?

With an anxious smile, he knelt down closer to her. "How do you know the name Silent Arrow?" he asked.

Trapped in a feverish stupor upon awakening again, all Shiona could comprehend was that her friend Silent Arrow had surely returned to help her. Yet she could not help but wonder why he would ask such a question about his own name.

A slight smile quivered across her face. "Silent . . . Arrow . . . ," she said in an almost whisper as she again felt sleep trying to claim her.

Shadow Bear was confused. He so badly wanted answers from her about his brother.

And where was the white man he had seen with her before the storm soldiers began throwing their dangerous spears from the sky? He wondered if she was from a soldier town, and if so, which one?

His scout had brought him news that the soldier town called Fort Chance was going to be abandoned, and surely was by now. Had those who lived at the soldier town also abandoned this woman?

Like Shadow Bear's brother, Silent Arrow, was this woman lost? Had the white man with her even abandoned her?

Shadow Bear was torn. Whites were guilty of stealing everything from the red man, a piece of ground at a time, a corner of his people's hearts at a time, and who needlessly killed the buffalo to keep the red man from having them.

It was his first instinct as a red man to leave the woman behind, yet he knew that he could not abandon someone who intrigued him so much.

And she was someone who surely somehow knew his brother, for as she opened her eyes, once again she suddenly spoke his brother's name and again reached out for Shadow Bear.

"How do you know the name Silent Arrow?" he again asked. "Do you know the man? Or only the name?"

But again she did not respond.

Her hand fell back down beside her on the blankets she lay upon as she again fell into a strange sort of sleep that he knew had to have been brought on by the fever that was ravaging her body and brain.

He gently drew the corners of the blankets more closely around her face, to give her as much warmth as possible from them, yet purposely kept her face visible enough for him still to gaze upon.

She made places inside his body come

alive that he had never been aware of before. Never in his life had he come face-to-face with such loveliness. And she seemed so tiny, so vulnerable, and was for certain so dangerously ill!

He again thought of how his grandmother had spoken of having seen a woman in her vision. What was the purpose of having seen this woman? Did it have to do with his brother?

"The only way I can know where or how she knew my brother, is to take her to my village and see that she is made well by my shaman . . . enough for her to speak truths to him, and to me," he whispered to himself.

He bent to lift her into his arms, but stopped and gasped when he saw two bloody halves of a broken arrow shaft.

"She must be wounded," he whispered in a panic. The fever that had her in such a deadly grip might have been caused by a wound made by an arrow.

The fact that the arrow had been removed made his heart skip a beat. Surely his brother had been with her long enough to perform that task.

He frowned as he examined the shaft of the arrow. He recognized the pattern — the same arrows had been found at the sites of other violent, pointless deaths. Whoever had shot her was the same person who left destruction behind everywhere he went.

Desperate now to see just how badly her wound was, Shadow Bear gently unwrapped the blanket from around the woman, his eyes searching for the place where the arrow had entered her lovely flesh.

But his eyebrows forked with question when he found that the only blood she had on her person was a few spots on her blouse and skirt.

He now knew that this woman was not the one shot by this arrow, which made him wonder then, who . . . ?

A panic grabbed at his heart. Perhaps Silent Arrow was the victim, and the woman had treated his injury before her illness got the better of her.

"My brother is out there somewhere, injured. Where did the arrow penetrate? Is he now dead . . . or alive?" he whispered harshly, his eyes now on the woman again.

Anxiously, Shadow Bear searched the cave flooring for signs of blood.

When he found it, his heart seemed to drop to his feet, for there was a lot of blood where his brother had surely lain as the woman had cared for the wound.

He followed the path of blood outside to where a lone horse grazed peacefully. Surely his brother had taken the other horse, the one on which the white man had ridden with the woman.

Had the white man cowardly left the white woman alone in the cave to fend for herself? Or had something happened to the white man before they arrived there?

Troubled by too many questions, and feeling desperate now to get the woman to his village, Shadow Bear rushed back into the cave and scattered dirt onto the flames of the fire, extinguishing it.

He looked around and saw the woman's personal bag. He knew she would need it, so he secured it to her horse, then returned and gently gathered the woman and the blankets into his arms.

In a half run, he took her to his steed, gently placed her on his saddle, making sure she was steady enough, then tied the reins of the lone horse to his own.

Finally, he mounted Star and, cradling the woman against his chest, he rode toward his camp as quickly as he dared.

CHAPTER 9

His tears must not disturb my heart,
But who shall change the years, and part
The world from every thought of pain?
— Alice Meynell

Everyone at his village watched as Shadow Bear carried a white woman into their shaman's tepee.

White Eagle quickly stood, his long and flowing gray hair hanging around his shoulders and down his back. "Who is this woman?" he asked, his leathery face proof of his seventy winters. "Why have you brought her to me?"

"She is in desperate need of your medicine," Shadow Bear said. He gently placed Shiona on the plush bed, then turned to his shaman again. "It is imperative that you get this woman well enough to awaken and talk, and quickly," he said tightly. "I have an important question that I must ask her. She must give me answers. I need these answers soon."

"Why is this woman of importance to you?" White Eagle asked, although it was not a normal thing to question a chief's decision.

But it was not a usual thing for his chief to demand help for any *washechus,* much less a white woman.

"What answers are you seeking from her?" White Eagle asked, this time more guardedly, as he went and stood at Shadow Bear's side and studied the face of the white woman.

He bent to his knees beside her and slowly drew back the blanket as he searched over her tiny body for signs of an injury. All that he saw was a slight bit of blood on her blouse and skirt, but none on her person.

He studied her face.

He could not help but see that it was a face of angelic beauty. She was as pale as winter snows, her thick lashes like long veils over her closed eyes.

His gaze went to her hair. Rarely had he seen hair of this golden color.

He could not help but lift a hand there and gently touch it, awed by its softness. All of his people's hair was raven black and

87

coarse to the touch.

Realizing that his chief was observing him closely, White Eagle slowly drew his hand away. Again he questioned Shadow Bear. "She is not injured?"

"*Ho,* yes, she has a fever," Shadow Bear said.

White Eagle gently placed his hand on her brow, then looked quickly up at Shadow Bear as he drew his hand away from the woman's hot flesh. "Do you know why she is ill with such a temperature?" he asked, searching his chief's eyes for answers his chief did not seem to want to tell him. "Has she possibly brought illness into our fold?"

"I do not know the reason, but I do know that you must medicate her and get her well enough to speak to me," Shadow Bear said. He knew that he risked the health of his village, but his need was too great to consider anything else.

"Why is it so important to you that she speaks to you?" White Eagle said, striding toward the far back of his lodge.

He selected a buckskin bag and carried it back to where Shiona lay.

"I do not know anything about her, not even her name, but I do know that she has knowledge of my brother. When I first found her, she spoke Silent Arrow's name to me more than once," Shadow Bear explained.

"I believe she was with my brother, and I think that she helped him. I found two bloody arrow shafts close to where she lay, and I cannot help but believe they came from my beloved brother's flesh."

"You followed your grandmother's instructions as to where she saw this woman in her vision and you found her?" White Eagle said, lifting the blankets away from Shiona.

"*Ho,* yes, I found her in a cave that my grandmother's vision led me to," Shadow Bear said. "There is always a purpose for her visions, so I knew it was important for me to find her."

White Eagle nodded as he then gently brushed some of Shiona's golden hair back farther from her face and brow. "Had you not been led to her, I doubt she would have been alive for much longer. I will medicate her to rid her of her fever, and then I will see that she is fed nourishing broth when she awakens."

"And so you do believe she will awaken?" Shadow Bear asked, gazing at Shiona, again taken by her innocent loveliness.

"If your grandmother's vision led you to this woman, and there was a purpose for you having found her, *ho,* I do believe she will awaken soon. My medicines and gentle caring for her will make it so. She will grow stronger and be a vital person again," White Eagle said, nodding.

"I need for her to awaken to speak to me as soon as possible," Shadow Bear stressed.

"Perhaps when she spoke his name to you, she thought it was Silent Arrow who she was addressing," White Eagle said.

Across her brow, he softly applied a white cream taken from the roots of various plants that were dug from the ground, mashed and cooked, and then made into a soft, thick liquid that would be easily applied to the one who was ill.

Then he took a cup and placed it gently to Shiona's lips, urging the liquid down her throat.

"*Ho,* yes, I believe when she saw me, she did think she was seeing Silent Arrow."

"She did not speak her name to you?" White Eagle asked.

"She was awake for only short intervals, and during her lucid periods, I tried to get answers from her."

"*Hau,* I will remain attentive to the woman. I will have her awake for you as soon as I can," White Eagle promised. He wiped Shiona's mouth clean with a soft ckskin cloth. "Patience is needed here,

90

my chief. Patience."

"I have learned the art of patience from the time I was old enough to know what the word meant," Shadow Bear said.

"I shall return soon. If she awakens, send word to me quickly," he said over his shoulder to the Shaman.

"I will do as much as I can for you," White Eagle promised.

Shadow Bear turned to him. "This is *wast-este*, good, for when you do this for me, you will also be doing it for my brother."

White Eagle nodded and turned toward Shiona as Shadow Bear stepped outside.

Shadow Bear dropped the entrance flap back down into place, then turned and started walking toward his home.

Suddenly he stopped. His breath caught. He could hardly believe his eyes.

His brother was there, alive!

He was on a steed unfamiliar to Shadow Bear and entering on the far side of the village.

Then his heart skipped a beat when he realized that something was very wrong with his brother.

As Shadow Bear watched, mortified, his brother slowly slumped over the strange horse. His face was flushed, as the white woman's had been.

It was evident that he was not well, either.

In his mind's eye he saw the two arrow halves in the cave, blood on them both.

He looked immediately at his brother's bare and broad muscled shoulders and chest. Alarm rushed through him when he saw the raw, puckered wound on his brother's shoulder. The wound was surely caused by the arrow that he had seen in the cave beside the ill woman.

He gasped and bolted forward when his brother slid from the horse, landing unconscious on the ground.

CHAPTER 10

. . . love me for love's sake, that evermore
Thou mayst love on, through love's eternity.

— Elizabeth Barrett Browning

Everyone who had caught sight of Silent
Arrow approaching had surrounded the two
brothers. Everything was quiet as Shadow
Bear placed a gentle hand on his brother's
cheek. "Silent Arrow . . . ? *Misun,* younger
brother?"

Silent Arrow awakened slowly and momentarily gazed into Shadow Bear's eyes.
"Shiona," he said softly. "Go . . ."

Shadow Bear's eyes widened in wonder of
who this Shiona might be, but before he
could question Silent Arrow he had closed
his eyes and was unconscious again.

Dancing Breeze slowly knelt down beside
Silent Arrow, her old, faded eyes filling with

tears as she studied her youngest grandson. Her gaze fell upon the puckered wound on his shoulder.

"He spoke a name to me and that was all he said," Shadow Bear said, slowly moving his hand from his brother's face.

"A name?" Dancing Breeze asked, forking a thick and shaggy eyebrow as she looked quickly over at Shadow Bear. "What name?"

"A strange one that I have never heard before," Shadow Bear said. "He spoke the name Shiona."

"Shiona . . . ?" Dancing Breeze said, again gazing at Silent Arrow.

"I must get him where he can be seen to," Shadow Bear said as he slid his arms beneath his brother, then gently lifted him.

He stood and walked slowly away from the wondering crowd, then stopped and looked at his grandmother, who remained beside him.

"Where shall I take him for his medicine?" he asked. The white woman still occupied the shaman's tent, and he did not want to move her to another lodge and risk spreading her illness among his people.

"Take your brother to my lodge," Dancing Breeze said, already turning toward her home. "The white woman of my vision must stay in one place until she awakens and

94

responds to questions that need answering."

Shadow Bear nodded.

As he carried his brother toward his grandmother's tepee, he again looked over at the shaman's. Inside that lodge was truly a woman of mystery, a woman who had spoken his brother's name while in her strange sort of stupor that was surely brought on by her fever. Had she helped his brother despite her illness? Was her name Shiona?

"Carry him with much ease to my bed of blankets," Dancing Breeze murmured as she placed a hand on her entrance flap and held it aside for Shadow Bear to enter. "I had not yet rolled my blankets up for the day before hearing of Silent Arrow's arrival home."

Shadow Bear nodded and went inside, easing his brother onto his grandmother's blankets, the fire warm on his back as he knelt down and studied his brother's wound.

"I shall prepare medicines for Silent Arrow," Dancing Breeze said, reaching for her husband's bag of medicines, which she had vowed to keep until she drew her last breath. She hoped that her chieftain grandson would claim the bag for himself, and then hand it down to his own son when he found the right woman to bear him that son.

"I do not like the way he still sleeps," Shadow Bear said thickly. "He should be awake. Look closely at his wound. Whoever doctored it did it skillfully. I know his injury is not what keeps him asleep. Then what might it be?"

Dancing Breeze leaned lower over Silent Arrow to take a better look at the puckered wound.

She turned and gazed into Shadow Bear's eyes. "It seems the right medicines were placed on your brother's shoulder," she said, frowning in wonder. "Who had such knowledge? Did a friend Lakota find him and minister to him?"

"I do not think so, or that friend would have brought him home to us," Shadow Bear said. He reached out and felt his brother's brow. "He is not feverish."

"I believe his need of sleep is from sheer exhaustion from finding his way home after having lost much blood from the wound," Dancing Breeze murmured. "I shall place additional medicine on his injury, then make his favorite soup, which he will have waiting for him when he chooses to awaken again."

Shadow Bear gazed toward the entrance flap, again thinking of someone beyond it, in another tepee.

The white woman.

Hopefully she would awaken soon and be able to answer questions.

He gazed at his brother again.

Or perhaps his brother would be the one to give him answers.

Only time would tell!

He gave his grandmother a hug, then rose and left the lodge.

As he stepped outside, he looked around him and found many of his people standing there, awaiting some word about Silent Arrow.

"My brother is not all that ill," he said, bringing sighs of relief from them all. "Most of his trouble comes from having lost much blood after having been wounded."

"How was he wounded? Who harmed him?" a voice from the crowd asked.

"I do not know who wounded him, but I can tell you that he was downed by the design of arrow that our enemies carry in their quivers," Shadow Bear said, once again in his mind's eye seeing the two shafts of the arrow in the cave with the white woman.

"I reassure you, my people, that my brother will be all right," Shadow Bear said. "Prayer will make it so! Go. Pray, as I go to my own lodge to say my own prayers."

He hurried into his tepee and sat down beside his lodge fire. He gazed into the slowly rolling flames, his mind a jumble of unanswered questions.

The white woman.

When he had first seen her, she had been with a white man.

Where was he now?

Would he eventually find his way to the Lakota village to claim her?

Would he bring trouble with him in the form of white pony soldiers?

Although Fort Chance was a thing of the past, were there not other soldier forts nearby?

He knew now that he could not rest until he had answers.

CHAPTER 11

I feel the bond of nature draw me to my
   own,
My own in thee, for what thou art is mine.
                              — John Milton

Shiona slowly awakened, aware of the
elderly man who sat beside her, his old, pale
brown eyes studying her.

There had been brief periods of lucidity
when she had listened to dialogue exchanged between those who came and
asked about her.

From the little she understood of their
language, she learned that this old man,
who had cared for her with such gentleness,
was White Eagle, and that he was a shaman.

Having listened as best she could through
her feverish state, she had learned that the
Indian who had saved her from a certain
death in the cave was a chief, for he had

been addressed as such more than once as he knelt beside her, studying her. But she had no idea yet where she was, or whose tribe she was among.

"You are awake," White Eagle said, slowly reaching a hand to her brow. "And you no longer have fever. That is good. You will soon be well."

"Thank you for caring for me while I've been so ill," Shiona murmured, slowly becoming more aware of things the longer she was awake.

She knew that she had some sort of soft gown on, surely made by skins of some animal, and that she smelled clean, which had to mean that someone bathed her.

She could not help but wonder who.

Had it been this shaman?

Or had a woman been assigned by him to do this?

She could even smell the sweetness of her hair, which meant someone had taken the time to wash it.

"It is my chief who asked me to care for you," White Eagle said, placing a log on the fire in his fire pit.

He then started to rise but her questions kept him there with her, and he felt that she deserved answers after having fought so hard to survive her illness.

"Where am I?" Shiona asked, weakly propping herself up on her elbow to look slowly around her. She saw all sorts of vials and bags, surely used while this shaman worked his miracles and magic on those who were ill. "Which tribe am I among?"

"You are among the Lakota people. You were found by my chief, whose name is Shadow Bear, in a cave while he was searching for his brother," White Eagle said softly. "He did not find his brother there, but instead found you, a white woman, who was delirious with fever."

Tears filled Shiona's eyes as she recalled that cave, and who was buried there.

She turned her eyes away from the shaman so that he would not see the tears she was fighting back. She did not want to explain those tears. She wanted no one but herself to know that she had buried her brother in the cave. It was her secret.

When she knew for certain that her eyes were dry again, she turned to White Eagle. "And so your chief brought me here," she said, vaguely remembering someone lifting her into his arms, and strangely enough remembering how clean he had smelled . . . like a mixture of spring winds and fresh, clean river water.

Through her haziness she did somehow

recall the handsomeness of the man who swept her into his arms, his midnight-dark eyes reflecting his concern.

She started to ask why he had troubled himself by saving a white woman when someone threw aside the entrance flap. Shadow Bear filled the entire entrance with his muscled body, the fire's glow reflecting on a face so handsome. Shiona was embarrassed when seeing him actually drew her breath away.

"My chief," White Eagle said as he rose and went to him. "The woman is awake. I will leave you alone."

Shadow Bear nodded, his eyes focused on Shiona, who now sat up, her golden hair long and flowing down her back, her skin almost as white as the doeskin gown she wore.

"Chief Shadow Bear, I want to thank you for saving me from what I know was certain death," Shiona said, breaking the silence between them. "I am almost certain I got ill from drinking the water in the cave. My horses were somewhat ill, too, from having drunk it."

"When I chose to bring you among my people, I knew the dangers because of your fever," Shadow Bear said, relief washing through him. Her illness would not spread

102

to his people.

"Then why did you bring me here?" Shiona asked softly, realizing how his nearness made her heart flutter.

She had never thought much about Indian warriors before, one way or another, whether or not they were handsome. She had just known to be wary of all Indians, for she knew how they resented white people.

She was truly confused by why she had been treated so kindly and gently by these Indians.

But now, as Chief Shadow Bear knelt across the fire from her, his chest bare, and wearing only a breechclout, she felt something besides apprehension, or fear.

She saw him as very kind and muscled . . . a desirable man.

Blushing, she turned her eyes away from him, then looked up when he asked her name.

"My name?" she murmured.

"You know my name is Shadow Bear, so I would like to know by what name you are called," he said warmly, his dark eyes searching hers.

"My name . . . I am called by the name . . . Shiona," she said shyly.

Shadow Bear tensed at her answer, recalling his brother's words. But he tried to hide his impatience so that he wouldn't frighten Shiona. He wanted to give her a chance to be open and honest with him.

He wanted her to trust him.

"Where is your family? Why were you alone in the cave?" he then asked. "Where is the man I saw you with the day before the fire came and turned the world of the Lakota black?"

Shiona's heart skipped a beat.

Was this young Indian chief setting a trap with his questions?

If he knew that she was totally alone in the world, what would that mean to him? What answers should she give him?

And now that she knew that he had seen her prior to her brother's death, Lord, for a moment she wondered if he had killed him.

Yet surely he hadn't been the one to have harmed her brother, or else why would he be curiously asking about him?

Unless it was a ploy to guide her away from casting blame on him or one of his warriors.

Could she be signing her own death warrant if she gave this man the wrong answers?

"Do not be afraid to speak answers to me when I ask you questions," Shadow Bear said. But his eyes were studying her closely, gauging her reactions. He wanted her to be innocent, but he was troubled that his brother had spoken her name, and she had not yet mentioned Silent Arrow.

"Shiona, where is your family?" he persisted. "Why were you alone in the cave? Where are you from? And what was that white man to you whom I saw you with?"

Realizing now that she had no other choice, Shiona knew that she must answer his questions. Had not his shaman taken care of her with such gentleness? She might not even be alive now had it not been for these people's generosity!

"I am all that is left of my family," Shiona said, her voice breaking as she lowered her eyes, the pain harsh inside her heart.

"And why is that?" Shadow Bear asked, kneeling beside her.

He was tempted to reach out and touch her hair, and then her face, but forced himself to refrain from such foolishness, for she was finally now trusting him enough to be open with him.

"You have not said yet why you are alone now, without family," Shadow Bear said gently, not wanting to upset her.

"I know you asked me a question, but it is something so hard to say," Shiona said, tears splashing from her eyes. "Please. I . . . I . . .

don't want to say any more about my family . . . my brother, my father . . . and my mother."

She just could not say the words he wanted to hear. Saying that her family was dead, aloud, would make it all too real.

He saw that she was struggling with her answers about her family. He saw how his questions had brought such pain into her eyes. That was answer enough. He knew now that she was a woman alone. He would find out why, and how, later.

"Is the name Silent Arrow familiar to you?" Shadow Bear asked, unable to delay any longer, for he knew now, without a doubt, that they had been in the cave together.

"Silent Arrow?" Shiona said, her eyes filled with question. "You have spoken the name another time to me. Why? Should I know the name? Should . . . I . . . know the one it belongs to?"

"Are you saying that you are not familiar with that name?" Shadow Bear asked, searching her eyes, his jaw tightening, for why would she not admit to having known his brother?

Was she hiding something?

When she saw his reaction Shiona felt fear for the first time in his presence.

The name Silent Arrow wasn't familiar to her!

She could not remember having ever known it.

Why was this chief asking about the name? What did it mean to him?

Should she know someone by that name?

If she let him know that she didn't know a Silent Arrow, would it change how Shadow Bear had been so kind to her?

"Silent Arrow is my brother," Shadow Bear said thickly. "He was missing, and when I found you in the cave, I also found a broken, bloody arrow beside you. Could it have come from my brother? Was he in that cave with you at some time?"

Now Shiona realized the importance of answering him correctly. It could even mean life or death for herself.

She saw a mixture of emotions in his eyes . . . a look of disappointment and mistrust.

Shadow Bear could not understand the game this woman was playing. If his brother had spoken her name, they had to have known each other.

Why then would she not say so?

He knew that none of this should be so important to him, yet it was. He was attracted to this woman, and he wanted her to be honest with him about everything.

Did she think that he would expect more of her where his brother's health had been concerned?

No.

None of this made sense.

But he wanted to give her the benefit of the doubt, and he would!

Shiona gazed at Shadow Bear with a wariness that she hoped he would not notice.

She knew now that she had no choice but to wait and see how he treated her after having not gotten the answers he expected from her. Would he send her away, to fend for herself, or continue to help her until she was strong enough to travel on her own again?

She eyed him with uncertainty when he placed a gentle hand at her elbow and helped her to her feet.

"Hakamya-upo," he said, his eyes locking with hers.

"I do not speak your language well, so I do not know what you just said to me," Shiona said guardedly.

"I said to come with me," he said. "I mean you no harm. Come."

Trembling, she did as he asked. She had no choice but to go with him, but where was he taking her?

When they stepped outside the shaman's lodge, for a moment the morning sun blinded her.

But as her eyes finally adjusted to the light, she looked slowly around her and saw the loveliness of the village, the tepees snow white, the people dressed in beautifully beaded clothes.

Several children ran up and gazed at her. She smiled at them, then walked ahead with Shadow Bear.

They were heading in the direction of a much larger tepee than the others, and she knew that she was being taken to the chief's lodge. Shiona wondered if that was good or bad.

CHAPTER 12

The angels, not half so happy in heaven,
Went envying her and me.
— Edgar Allan Poe

"Where are you taking me?" Shiona could not help but ask as she still gazed intently at the larger tepee. She gave him a pensive look. "Are you taking me to your home?"

"*Ho,* yes, and again I tell you that you have nothing to fear," Shadow Bear said. "Since you are feeling so much better, you do not need to stay with the shaman. He has made you well enough to live elsewhere. And it is best that his dwelling is always free for my people, should any of them need his medicine."

"I see," Shiona murmured.

She was torn and confused. Did he actually plan to keep her there, in the small confines of a tepee, with him? Wouldn't they have to sleep too close to each other? In her world, the men and women never lived together until vows were spoken.

But she was in Shadow Bear's world now. And despite her misgivings, she was attracted to this man more than any man before him. No white man could compare with this chief's handsomeness. And she had never met anyone who carried himself as though he actually amounted to something as did this Indian chief.

And his eyes!

When she gazed into his midnight-dark eyes, she was taken aback, for she saw a man who was intrigued by her.

As they walked across the grounds of the village, past one tepee after another, Shiona tried to focus her attention on something other than her nervousness, and stole a glance at Shadow Bear. His sleekly muscled body rippled as he walked, his power echoing within his long strides.

Gleaming in the sunlight, his long black hair lifted with each step, a fancy headband holding it back from his brow, a feather in the back tied in a loop.

Afraid he might catch her looking at him, she turned her eyes quickly from him.

Again she thought of where life had brought her.

She was truly alone in this world.

Yes, she had kin back in Kansas City, but none who had ever been close to her and her family, for her father had traveled around too much for them to keep in touch. Her family's lives had centered around the forts her father was stationed at. She would just get used to being at one fort when her father would be assigned elsewhere, where his skills were needed.

It had been a lonely world, where Shiona could never trust making a special bond with someone else of her own age, for more than likely they would not know each other for very long.

So for now, Shiona truly had no idea what she was going to do once Shadow Bear said that she could go.

She gave him another sidewise glance, wondering why he hadn't mentioned her leaving. Surely he did not plan to make her stay there. Surely he did not look to her now as a captive . . . his captive.

In time she would know, but just how much time would it take for him to share his decision with her?

Sighing, she centered her attention elsewhere, away from the handsome Lakota chief who walked beside her. She was intrigued by several old men sitting around

112

the huge outdoor fire, each of their lips tugging at their own long-stemmed pipes of stone as their eyes now followed her.

Conscious of their stares, she looked somewhere else and saw that the village was an island of green, it seemed, where the recent fire had not reached.

She saw where some tepees had been somehow scorched by the fire, but had not been leveled by it. She saw strings of smoke rising from the cooking fires within the lodges of the village, twisting into the air and sending off tantalizing aromas that made her belly ache with hunger. Up until today, she had not eaten much at all since she came down with the fever.

She vaguely recollected, somehow, the shaman having spoon-fed her broth, but now she was starting to feel weak from a combination of hunger and the lingering effects of her illness.

Still, she knew that in a matter of days she would be as good as new, for she had always bounced back from illnesses so quickly. It had surprised both her mother and her father, and especially the doctors who were taking care of her, how strong she truly was, when in truth she looked as though she could not fend for herself against even a small housefly!

Suddenly Shiona went cold through and through and her steps faltered when she saw someone familiar to her in this Lakota village! She had spotted the old woman who had appeared to her in a dream when she was delirious with fever in the cave. The elderly woman was sitting on the ground with a small stick in her hand, drawing designs on the earth seemingly telling a story to a group of children clustered around her, who were listening intently to what she was saying.

She was stunned to know that the person who had come to her in her dream, who had sung to her, who had bathed her brow, who had spoken so kindly to her, was real!

And she was actually there in the Lakota village.

The mystery of how this had happened made goose bumps crawl along Shiona's flesh.

A part of her wanted to run over to the elderly lady and see if she recognized her. Yet a part of her that was afraid of the truth of the dream kept her away from the temptation of seeking truths from her.

Shadow Bear had seen the alarm in Shiona's eyes and how her footsteps had faltered upon seeing Shadow Bear's grandmother, and he understood why she was stunned. Surely Shiona had been aware of his grandmother when they met in her vision. Shiona must believe the entire episode was a dream.

"Let us go on to my lodge," Shadow Bear gently encouraged as he took Shiona by an elbow and led her away.

"The woman," Shiona said, looking into Shadow Bear's eyes. "Who is that woman?"

"She is my grandmother," Shadow Bear replied, watching her reaction, seeing the wonder of all of this leap into Shiona's eyes.

"Your . . . grandmother . . . ?" Shiona said, trying to hide her true wonder of the moment.

"*Ho,* yes, my grandmother," Shadow Bear said.

He didn't offer any more information. If Shiona were to ask how it could have happened that she had been visited by his grandmother in such a way, he knew that there was nothing he could say to make her understand the magic of his grandmother. He sometimes did not understand it himself.

"We are at my lodge now," Shadow Bear said, stepping away from her and holding the entrance flap aside for her. "Go inside. I have prepared a warm fire and there are soft pelts upon which you can sit."

Shiona stepped inside the tepee. A swift examination of the interior convinced her that a single man occupied the tepee. Clearly the handsome young Lakota chief was not married, nor did he have any children.

She knew that understanding this should mean absolutely nothing to her, yet it did. It made a sensual thrill swim at the pit of her stomach to know that he was a man who was surely seeking the right woman to have as his wife, for no man as virile as she knew this man must be, stayed alone for long.

The thought of him taking her into his arms and kissing her swept through her consciousness, again causing a sweet, warm weakness at the pit of her stomach. She hastily pushed those thoughts aside, for she knew that they were absolutely forbidden, and also, she was in no position to daydream about such a thing, much less expect it to one day truly happen!

"Sit," Shadow Bear said, leading her toward the soft pelts. "For now, consider this your home. This is where you will eat and sleep until another lodge can be readied for you. A sleeping bag is behind you."

"Thank you," Shiona said, trying to calm her anxiety.

Would he take advantage of her?

"Clothes and food will be brought to you," Shadow Bear said, watching how the fire's glow played on this woman's lovely, pale skin, making a hunger rush to his loins that hardly ever happened. He usually had full control of his emotions and needs.

But while he was around this woman, he found the control of his emotions and needs battling him, heart and soul.

"Thank you," Shiona said, seeing something in the depths of his eyes as he gazed at her that made her insides tremble with needs she had never felt before.

But she had never been in the presence of such a man before.

She smiled bashfully up at him from where she sat; then she sighed heavily when he suddenly turned and walked from the tepee, leaving her alone with the fire and her thoughts. But just as she started to relax, she spotted Shadow Bear's weapons, which included several bows painted various ways and a quiver of arrows.

Shocked out of her reverie, she hurried to the back of the tepee where the arrows were in the quiver. She grabbed one and studied the designs. She trembled with relief when she found none that shared the deadly design of the arrows that had killed her family.

She walked slowly around Shadow Bear's tepee, brushing her hands along various things that she knew he must have touched himself. The more she touched, the more she knew that she was smitten, totally smitten, by a man she could never forget.

She gazed at the rolled-up blankets and pelts alongside the walls of the tepee. Surely among those were ones he used for his bed . . . and ones she would use for hers!

She looked around at the small spaces of the tepee and wondered how in the world they could both sleep in the same lodge without almost touching while they slept!

Chapter 13

And this maiden she lived with no other
  thought
Than to love and be loved by me.
                    — Edgar Allan Poe

Shadow Bear knew that Silent Arrow must
have awakened and was well on the road to
recovery, or Dancing Breeze would not have
been outside with the children this morning. He headed toward her lodge where his
brother was to stay until he was totally well
because he wanted to find out if he was well
enough to walk to Shadow Bear's lodge. If
he could, then Shadow Bear would soon
have the answers he could not get from the
white woman.

He stepped inside his grandmother's
tepee, where he immediately saw Silent Arrow sitting beside the fire on thick, rich
pelts, eating a bowl of soup.

Although the recent days had been warm, the storm had brought with it a cooling that everyone appreciated, but that required fires in all the lodges.

"*Misun,* my brother, it is good to see you are so much better," Shadow Bear said, bending and giving his brother an affectionate hug.

"It is good that you are here," Silent Arrow said, returning the hug. When Shadow Bear stepped away, Silent Arrow studied him. "I sense that something else besides your younger brother has brought you to our grandmother's lodge this morning," he said.

Silent Arrow set his empty bowl aside as Shadow Bear sat on pelts opposite the fire from him. "Shadow Bear, I do see something in your eyes and expression that I find hard to interpret, whereas usually I can read you very well," he said, searching his brother's face.

"This morning, my brother, I have someone on my mind," Shadow Bear said gravely.

"Someone?" Silent Arrow said, forking an eyebrow. He drew a blanket more snugly around his bare shoulders, where his grandmother's medicine had dried around the pucker of his arrow wound. "Could this someone be a woman? Have you finally found one that mystifies you?"

"*Ho,* yes, she mystifies me very much," Shadow Bear said softly. "Do you feel strong enough to walk to my tepee with me?"

"I am strong enough, *ho,* but why are you asking this of me?" Silent Arrow said, puzzled by his brother's strange behavior.

"You will know soon," Shadow Bear said. "Do not do this only because I am asking this of you. Come with me only if your legs are strong enough to carry you there."

"My legs are strong enough," Silent Arrow said, yet he groaned when he pushed himself up from the pelts, only now realizing how these past days had taken so much from him. He had been perhaps the strongest warrior, next to his brother, of the warriors of their Grey Owl Band of Lakota.

Seeing how his brother wobbled as he struggled to get to his feet, Shadow Bear went quickly to him. He placed a gentle arm around his brother's waist. "If this is too soon for you to walk as far as my tepee, I trust that you would say so," he said anxiously.

"Whatever your reason for urging me to accompany you to your lodge, it must be of great importance to you, or you would not ask this of me. And, *ho,* yes, Brother, I would tell you if I were unable to go with you," Silent Arrow said.

He turned to Shadow Bear. "My chieftain brother, do I have to wait until we get inside your lodge for me to know why I am asked to go there?" Silent Arrow asked, almost guardedly.

"Someone is at my lodge whom I want you to meet," Shadow Bear blurted out, knowing it was wrong not to tell his brother the reason he was taking him from his sickbed, yet seeing the need to do it in this way. He did not want to mention Shiona's name to his brother before he saw Silent Arrow's reaction to seeing her.

"Someone?" Silent Arrow inquired.

"*Ho,* yes, someone," was all that Shadow Bear replied.

If Shiona reacted when she saw Silent Arrow, as he was afraid that she might, then he would know that for some reason she was a woman of deceit where his brother was concerned.

He had to test this woman in order to know whether or not he should take her to a white man's fort, or ask her to stay longer among his people. And with him.

"I see that you, for whatever reason, would rather not speak a name, so I will not ask you to, but it is quite mysterious, my brother, how you are behaving today," Silent

Arrow said, stepping on outside with Shadow Bear.

The sun momentarily blinded Silent Arrow, and then his eyes grew used to the glare and he saw his grandmother rising from where she had sat among the children. She had told him that she would be just outside if he needed her.

A woman of such good heart, she had wanted to spend time with the children in order to make them understand that all was still well with the world even though the fire had come and destroyed so much of its beauty.

In a sense, the fire had been a blessing, for it had given his grandmother a reason to leave her lodge. Since the death of her husband and son, she had spent too much time alone in her tepee, continuing to mourn her losses.

When the children who had been listening to her stories saw that Silent Arrow was well enough to have left his grandmother's lodge, they all ran to him, squealing and touching him, obviously happy to see that he was all right. Then the two brothers proceeded to Shadow Bear's lodge.

When they reached their destination, Shadow Bear swept his entrance flap aside. He was anxious to gauge Shiona's reaction to seeing Silent Arrow, so he stepped farther into the lodge in order for his eyes to watch her as Silent Arrow stepped inside.

The moment Shiona saw Silent Arrow she recognized him. She now remembered having helped him. She had removed the arrow from his body.

Her eyes went quickly to where his wound was hidden beneath a blanket.

She could not help but wonder how it had healed.

She was glad to see that he was all right, but was puzzled by how both he and Shadow Bear were standing there, momentarily at a loss for words.

But the moment seemed more significant than that as her gaze met and held with Shadow Bear's.

She was taken aback by how intently he studied her, as though he had expected some sort of reaction from her when she saw Silent Arrow. She stiffened when she remembered the times he had spoken Silent Arrow's name to her and she had not been able to remember him.

Suddenly she realized how the fever had affected her. It had kept her from recalling things as she should have. She recalled how only moments ago Shadow Bear had actually been questioning her about Silent Arrow, whether or not she knew him. At that moment, she hadn't.

But seeing him now had made it all come back to her . . . how she found him with the terrible arrow in his shoulder, and how they had bonded as friends so quickly. He had trusted her enough to ask her to remove the arrow shaft from his shoulder.

Silent Arrow's eyes widened when he saw just who was sitting in his brother's lodge. It was the woman who had removed the arrow from his body and had applied medicines that he had prepared to his wound.

He also recalled how he had left her alone, feverish and in a deep sleep, and had fled on one of her horses. He had not been able to forget having done such a cowardly thing, yet had he not returned home when he had, for the care his injured body needed, he might not be alive today. He was enormously relieved to see that she was all right.

He hurried to Shiona and fell to his knees beside her. Without further thought, he wrapped her in his arms as the blanket fell away from his shoulders.

"I am so glad to see that you are all right," Silent Arrow said. "I should not have left you."

"But I am all right, thanks to Shadow Bear," Shiona said, gazing over Silent Ar-

125

row's shoulder up at Shadow Bear.

She saw so much in his eyes that she could not interpret, but mainly she saw mistrust.

He had questioned her about Silent Arrow and she had said she did not know of him. Oh, surely he saw her as a liar, or someone who might have cause to deceive him with wrong answers.

"Until I saw you now I . . . I . . . did not remember having ever been with you," Shiona said, easing away from Silent Arrow's embrace, yet her eyes still on Shadow Bear. "But now I do recall you, everything about you, and how I treated your wound."

She examined the puckered wound, smiling at Silent Arrow as she slowly touched it. "I am so glad that I was able to help you," she murmured. "Do not feel cowardly for having left me. Surely had you not returned home when you did you would have died. I could not have helped you any more. I fell into an unconscious state. I had hallucinations. I was so feverish."

She shifted her eyes to Shadow Bear again. "Then Shadow Bear found me and brought me to your village," she said, her voice breaking. "I will never be able to repay him enough for what he did for me."

She rose slowly and stood before Shadow Bear. "I do appreciate so much what you have done for me," she said. "And I am so glad that you brought Silent Arrow here this morning so that we could become reacquainted. I imagine a part of my memory was blocked from me because of the fever, but now that I have seen Silent Arrow, I truly remember him now."

Shadow Bear had witnessed this sort of thing more than once; how someone could be traumatized by one thing or another, especially a high fever, and forget things they would normally remember.

It was a great relief to know the woman was honest in all things that had concerned him. And the fact that he had doubted her so much made him feel guilty, for she had truly not given him any cause for mistrusting her.

"It is good that you remember things now," Silent Arrow said, drawing the blanket back around his shoulders, then rising to his feet and standing beside Shadow Bear. "And it is good that my brother found you and brought you home with him."

Silent Arrow reached a gentle hand to Shiona's arm. "What are your plans now?" he asked. "Where is your family?"

Having already placed doubt about herself inside Shadow Bear's mind and heart,

Shiona knew that full honesty was needed now.

"I truly thank you for your generosity. You have been more than kind to me, and I shall forever be in your debt." She searched Shadow Bear's eyes. "I feel now is the time for you to know as much about me as I can reveal. My tale might interest you," she murmured.

She paused, since she knew that her father was hated by the red man, and when they heard her story it might change their feelings about her. But she saw no choice but to be honest with Shadow Bear.

"My entire family is dead," Shiona said, swallowing hard, for to say it brought it all back. It was as though it was all new to her again, so raw, it made her heart ache.

"My father died first," she continued, brushing tears from her eyes. "My father. I am certain you knew him."

"His name?" Shadow Bear asked, seeing how difficult it seemed to be for her to reveal these things to him.

"My father's name?" Shiona asked, her eyes wavering. She lowered them momentarily, then looked into Shadow Bear's eyes again. "My father was Colonel Fred Bramlett of Fort Chance."

She saw an instant hate in both brothers'

eyes. She knew that her father was hated throughout the Indian world, and sometimes even among his own men. He was a man who had demanded discipline of his men, and a man who saw the Indians as murdering savages.

"My father died by an arrow such as I took from your shoulder, Silent Arrow," Shiona blurted out. "And my mother was killed the same way, with the same type of arrow, as was my brother." Her voice cracked with emotion.

"Shadow Bear, that day you saw me riding with a man, the man you have questioned me about?" she said. "That was my brother, Seth. He was dead shortly after you saw us together."

Shiona stifled a sob behind a hand. "My mother was murdered by renegades as she rode in a stagecoach away from Fort Chance, to return to Missouri, where our family had planned to establish a home again after the death of my father. But that is never to be now. I am alone in the world. I do not see why I was spared while my other loved ones died."

Hearing the despair in her voice, and feeling guilty for having ever doubted her, Shadow Bear reached for Shiona and drew her into his gentle embrace. "You are no longer alone," he assured her.

Shadow Bear's embrace told her that through all of his mistrust and doubts of her, he had found a way to care about her.

"You can stay . . . ," Shadow Bear began, then was interrupted by a woman's voice outside the lodge.

"It is my woman, Moon Glow," Silent Arrow said, a broad smile on his face. He stepped away from Shadow Bear and Shiona and held the entrance flap aside for Moon Glow to enter.

Moon Glow's face beamed as she stepped inside and saw Silent Arrow. She knew that he had been strong enough to have walked from his lodge to his brother's.

"I have brought food for the three of you. And clothes for the white woman," she said, unable to take her eyes off the man she loved, so glad that he had come through his injury all right.

Shiona could tell that Silent Arrow and the beautiful young maiden were madly in love. And when Silent Arrow took the heavy tray of food from her, although she knew his wound must ache from doing so, Shiona had no doubt how they both felt for each other.

Shiona noticed something else. The woman had a beautiful buckskin dress draped over one arm and when she came to Shiona, she handed it to her.

"Dancing Breeze asked me to bring this dress to you," Moon Glow murmured. "It is a dress recently made by me. It is now yours."

Shiona gasped, in awe of the lovely bead-work. "Thank you," she said, gently taking the dress from Moon Glow. "I truly love it."

"I will bring moccasins for you soon, too," Moon Glow said softly, her gaze moving to Shiona's hair, fascinated by its color. She reached out and touched it. "So pretty." Then she smiled into Shiona's eyes. "I have a red ribbon that would be pretty in your hair. Would you accept it as a gift from me if I brought it to you?"

Shiona was taken aback by this woman's generosity and wasn't sure what to say. Surely the ribbon was valuable to Moon Glow, so should she accept it and leave Moon Glow without it? Or might it be an insult to turn down such a gift?

"Shiona would be very pleased to have the ribbon," Shadow Bear said quickly on Shiona's behalf, for he could see Shiona's confusion, and understood.

Obviously pleased, Moon Glow nodded, gazed into Silent Arrow's eyes again, blushed, then turned and ran from the tepee.

Shadow Bear was so glad to finally know the truth about Shiona, and he now felt free to pursue the beautiful white woman's affection. She was a white woman, *ho,* but a white woman with a heart, for had she not tended to a red man's injuries without question?

He saw her as very special, indeed, yet that part of him that never trusted whites urged him to reserve a small corner of his heart wary of her because of who her father was, a man hated by all redskins, until she had proven to be honest in every way.

"The food smells and looks good, does it not?" Shadow Bear said, taking the tray from his brother and sitting it on the bulrush mats close to the fire pit.

Shiona nodded and smiled and settled in beside the fire with both handsome Lakota men after Shadow Bear brought wooden dishes from his supplies at the back of his lodge.

"The venison is tasty, do you not think so?" Shadow Bear asked Shiona as he gave her a slow smile. She nodded and continued to eat more than he had ever seen a woman eat before.

Until now she had seemed hesitant to eat

very much, but it seemed all tensions and reservations that had been there, between them, because of his foolish mistrust of her, were gone.

There was an air of lightheartedness in the tepee now, and it was heightened by the joyous shouts of the children outside, where the day was new and beautiful and filled with hope.

"My brother, where did you leave the offering to the buffalo?" Shadow Bear asked, wiping grease from his lips.

"Much farther than I should have," Silent Arrow said, giving his brother a knowing look. "Had I not gone there, I would not have made such an easy target for my enemy, who shot me and left me for dead. But it was the highest point I could find, a better place, I had thought, for the buffalo to hear my offering prayers to them."

"You have no idea who shot you?" Shadow Bear asked, glancing at Shiona.

He saw the pain in her eyes and now wished he had not brought up the subject of the arrow, as he had.

But he had to know who was roaming this land with a quiver full of such arrows, for who was to know who the next target might be?

"None at all," Silent Arrow said grudgingly. "Whoever did this seemed to have taken wing and flown quickly away."

"One day the culprit will be found and die by an arrow himself, for I shall be the one who shoots it into his heart," Shadow Bear said gruffly.

Just then Moon Glow stepped gingerly into the tepee. "I have brought the ribbon," she said, taking it to Shiona. "May I tie it into your hair?"

"It is so beautiful, Moon Glow, and yes, please do place it in my hair." Shiona was glad that Moon Glow had chosen this very moment to enter the lodge, for her presence brought everything within it a feeling of lightheartedness again, whereas only moments ago the topic had made the world turn suddenly bleak.

Moon Glow swept Shiona's hair back into a ponytail, then tied the bow around it.

Moon Glow stepped back, clasped her hands together, and sighed. "The red against the gold is so beautiful," she said, her eyes wide.

"*Ho,* so beautiful," Shadow Bear said, longing to be alone with Shiona, but this time in a much different way than ever before!

CHAPTER 14

My love is such that Rivers cannot quench,
Nor ought but love from thee give recompense.

— Anne Bradstreet

Shiona was awakened with a start from a deep yet peaceful sleep by the music of drums and rattles being played and the sounds of laughter. She sat up quickly and gazed overhead through the smoke hole and saw the blue sky.

A splash of sun warmed her face, alerting her that it was surely midmorning. She was stunned that she had not awakened earlier, yet the more she thought about it, she was able to understand.

After dinner, she and Shadow Bear had left his tepee and joined a group outside beside the huge outdoor fire and listened to stories being told by an elderly man late into the night.

She had been tired, but had not wanted to go to bed, especially after realizing that Shadow Bear might have feelings for her that matched her own for him.

He had expressed them in the way he had treated her all evening: so gentle, so caring. He had even sat her by his side on the chief's platform, where they had attracted many questioning stares.

After the stories were finished, Shadow Bear had escorted her back to his lodge. To secure her privacy, she had slept behind a blanket that Shadow Bear had hung on a rope from one side of the lodge to the other.

But last night, she had ached to have that blanket removed. She had wanted nothing more than to fall into the arms of a man she knew she would love forever.

Yet feeling brazen for such thoughts, she had hurried behind the blanket and plopped down onto the bed of pelts, without even first removing her clothes.

Everything had changed between them, which made Shiona somewhat awkward in his presence.

She had hurried behind the blanket so quickly last night she had no idea what was to happen today, for no one had told her.

"Are you awake?"

136

Shadow Bear's voice from beyond the blanket made Shiona's face grow hot with a blush, for just hearing it made her feel strangely warm inside, and she wondered if she would be able to be with him today without him reading her feelings.

Yet what would be the harm in that if he did?

She loved him and she hoped that he loved her, at least just a little bit!

"Yes, I am awake," she answered, reaching quickly up and touching her hair.

She groaned to herself as she felt how tangled her hair had become during her sleep. She glanced sideways and saw the lovely red ribbon lying inches from her head, where it had fallen off during the night.

She would never forget the sweetness of Moon Glow for offering her such a gift. She knew that those types of things did not come easy for the Indian nation, gotten usually only by trading for them.

"Are you dressed?" Shadow Bear asked.

He was able to see her shape through the blanket as she stood up.

He had hated parting from her last night when she had slipped behind the blanket without him. He had so badly wanted to hold her all through the night. He needed her as he had needed, or wanted, no other woman before her. His loins ached even now with the thought of what it would be to hold her and take her to his bed.

He knew that he should not allow his mind to wander to such places as that, not until they had professed their love for each other, which he knew would come soon, for he did love her and he could tell that she had such feelings for him, as well.

"Am I dressed?" Shiona said, laughing softly as she looked down at her wrinkled skirt and blouse. "In a sense, yes, I am dressed."

"You are not wearing the dress that Moon Glow gave to you," Shadow Bear said, his eyes widening when he heard a gasp from behind the blanket.

"How do you know that?" Shiona asked, her eyes wide.

Realizing that he had been caught, Shadow Bear was at a loss as to what to say back to her. "Today is a good day," he said, instead. "Come beyond the blanket. I have food for you. While we eat together I shall explain what is happening outside, for you surely hear the music and laughter."

"Yes, I hear it," Shiona said. She quickly raked her fingers through her hair, hoping to remove some of the tangles.

She glanced at a brush made by someone of his village out of porcupine quills, strange in its looks, and all bristly to her scalp when she used it.

Feeling presentable enough, though her clothes were terribly wrinkled, she timidly swept aside the blanket and stepped beyond it, where Shadow Bear stood, holding a tray of food.

"Good morning," Shiona murmured, wishing she didn't feel so shy now in his presence.

"Sit with me and eat as I describe the activities planned for today," Shadow Bear said, placing the tray of food on a bulrush mat beside the slowly burning fire in the fire pit.

He motioned with a hand toward a blanket and nodded toward it.

His silent message was quite clear to Shiona.

She smiled sweetly at him and sat down on one side of the tray of food as he settled down on the other side.

"It looks delicious," Shiona said, hoping he didn't hear her belly growl as the food's aroma wafted up.

"There is meat, fruit, and small cakes, all prepared for us by Moon Glow," Shadow Bear said. "I assure you that it is all good.

Moon Glow is going to make my brother a very good wife. She can cook, she can sew, and she knows which herbs to dig for in the woods. She can also tan clothes to perfection." He smiled. "I am saying too much about another lady."

"No, you're not," Shiona said.

She blushed as his gaze stayed on her face for too long. He seemed to be looking at her as if to memorize her!

"It is wonderful how Moon Glow knows all of these things and, yes, your brother is very lucky," Shiona murmured. "I only hope that I can learn some of those things, myself, for you see, I am from a military family. Most food was prepared for us, and we bought our clothes."

"Then what did you and your mother do to pass the time of day?" Shadow Bear asked, searching her eyes. He plucked a piece of bread up from the tray, as she did the same.

"I embroidered sometimes, but my joy came from reading books," Shiona said, searching the food for what to choose. She picked up a round cake that seemed to have some sort of nuts cooked in it.

"I have always wondered about what is inside the talking leaves," Shadow Bear said, slowly chewing on the bread, his eyes never leaving her, for as each moment passed, he was more entranced by her loveliness.

"Talking leaves?" Shiona asked, raising an eyebrow. "What is that?"

Shadow Bear laughed softly. "You call talking leaves by the name 'book,' " he said.

Then he heard some young girls singing outside, where the celebration was soon to start, in unison with the rhythmic beats of the drums and rattles. "We must hurry," he said.

He grabbed a piece of meat and shoved it in his mouth before rising to his feet.

"What is all of the excitement about outside your tepee?" Shiona asked, aware of the singing and how even more laughter filled the air.

"I should have told you last night, but you were so tired, I instead urged you to go on to your bed," Shadow Bear said.

He opened the flap and looked out at a group of young boys who were running around, laughing and playing tag with one another. He turned back to Shiona and knelt at her side, his eyes now level with hers. "There is to be a celebration today of my brother's homecoming and his improved health. You will join the celebration, will you not? You do need to be a part of it, you know. If not for you, who knows where my brother might be, or if he would even be alive?"

He reached a hand out for her and gently touched her face. He instantly felt the heat of a blush as her face turned a slight pinkish color.

"And I want you to see the goodness of my people," he said. "A people who see war with whites as bad. We seek peaceful ways as solutions for things. That is why we are still on land that has been my people's from the beginning of time."

"I would love to join the celebration," Shiona said, keenly aware of his hand on hers. The warmth of his flesh against hers sent spirals of desire into her heart.

Seeing much in her violet eyes he took one of her hands and helped her stand before him. He then swept his arms around her waist and drew her close. "Perhaps it is wrong, but I care deeply for you," he said thickly, their eyes locked and holding.

"Why do you think it is wrong to care for me?" Shiona asked.

It was a magical moment for her, a moment she had wished for after realizing just how much she did care for this handsome Lakota chief.

"You are a white woman; I am an Indian," Shadow Bear said huskily. "It is forbidden among your people to care for a man of my skin color. Knowing this, I have tried to ward off thoughts of you every time they came to me, but I can no longer do this. You are in my heart to stay. Do you want it to be there? Do you care as much for me as I care for you? I feel it in your embrace and I see it in your eyes that you do."

"I don't see how it can happen so quickly, but yes, I do care so much for you," Shiona said, trembling with excitement.

"Do you want me?"

"Yes, I so badly want you." She lowered her eyes timidly, then looked slowly into his midnight-dark eyes again. "But isn't it too soon?" she murmured. "We . . . scarcely know each other."

"In time we will know everything about each other, for you are going to stay among my people, are you not?" he said. "You have nowhere to go, no one to go to. There is only myself and my people. I want you. Please say that you will stay. Please say that you will be my woman."

"Nothing could drag me away," Shiona said, laughing softly when she saw his reaction to her words. "I mean to say I truly do want to stay . . . I truly do want to be your woman."

He lowered his lips to hers in a soft,

wondering kiss. Shiona twined her arms around his neck and pressed her body into his, feeling a passion she had never known possible.

But afraid of how quickly things were evolving with them, and not wanting to look brazen in this man's eyes, she stepped slowly away from him. "Shouldn't I get ready for the celebration?" she asked breathlessly, her heart pounding.

For the first time in her life she actually wanted a man and all that he could give her. She ached in parts of her body that she had never known could have feelings, much less such sensual and sweet feelings as had been brought on by Shadow Bear's kiss and embrace.

"Would you wear the dress that Moon Glow brought to you, as well as the moccasins?" Shadow Bear asked, reaching for and holding her hands. "Will you wear the red ribbon in your hair again? That would sorely please not only Moon Glow but also myself."

"Yes, I shall wear all that Moon Glow gave me," Shiona said softly.

"I do not know how you can be more beautiful than you are now, but I am certain you will be," Shadow Bear whispered.

"Shadow Bear?"

Moon Glow's voice from outside the closed entrance flap drew Shiona and Shadow Bear apart.

Shiona looked questioningly at Shadow Bear.

"Moon Glow has brought water for your hair," Shadow Bear explained. "She is going to wash it for you, and then if you wish, she will bring another basin of water for your bath. But for every bath after that, you will join the women as they go daily to the river."

"I look forward to learning all of your people's customs," Shiona said.

"I will leave now," Shadow Bear said, shoving aside the entrance flap and stepping outside before Moon Glow entered.

And when she did, Shiona blushed, for she was afraid that the lovely woman would see clean through her and know that she had only moments ago been kissed by her chief!

"I have brought warm water of yucca suds for your hair," Moon Glow said, smiling softly at Shiona. "It will make your golden hair shine."

"Thank you so much for everything." Shiona was so glad that she had such a friend already in Moon Glow. That would make her adjustment so much easier as she became a part of the Lakota world.

And then there was Shadow Bear!

How she looked forward to what he was going to teach her!

CHAPTER 15

If so I mourn, he weeps with me,
And where I am, there will he be.
                    — Thomas Lodge

The sun was high and bright. The air was
scented with the aroma of various foods
cooking, and the celebration for Silent Arrow's safe return home continued into the
afternoon.

Fat hump ribs were roasting over the fire,
sending their own tantalizing aromas sky-
ward, and various other foods had been
enjoyed during the day.

Shiona had watched as the intestines of a
buffalo that one warrior had chanced to find
were thoroughly cleaned by his wife, looped
over the end of a stick and roasted to a
crispy brown over the hot, outdoor fire.

Another woman had made her meat more
enticing, their strips having been braided

147

and looped in a chain stitch before putting it in the flames of the fire for roasting.

Moon Glow had told Shiona that meat roasted over a fire was wholesome and that the ashes that touched the outside were not injurious to the meat, but cleansing and stimulating to the system.

Shiona had grimaced at learning that the brains of animals were used to thicken soup, and that tripe, either boiled or roasted, was a favorite dish.

She knew now that meat was the main article of food for the Lakota. It was their staff of life and eaten at all meals.

Soup was their universal dish.

She had enjoyed all the varieties of meat, corn, and even squash as big as the paunch of a buffalo, all very rich and sweet from the hot ashes of the fire. She was comfortably full now, sitting with Dancing Breeze instead of Shadow Bear because he was involved in gambling games with his warriors. She had not been pleased by the presence of a man she despised who sat beside Shadow Bear, laughing and gambling with him.

He had come by invitation of Shadow Bear, but Shiona felt that Shadow Bear surely had no idea of the sort of man he was. She understood very well how scheming and disreputable this Frenchman, Pierre DuSault, was. Her father had dealt with him many times, and only at the start had their meetings been based on friendship.

Before Shiona's father had discovered the sort of man that he was, Pierre had invited her father and his family to his large expanse of a villa that sat across and downriver from the fort, midway between the Lakota village and Fort Chance.

After Shiona had seen this man's vast, expensive furniture and home, she had immediately thought that this man had somehow gotten most of it illegally.

Her father had been suspicious, too, after having seen it, and had quit associating with him, especially after Pierre made an aggressive pass toward Shiona. He had actually groped a breast through her dress as he asked her if she ever felt naughty.

After Shiona had disclosed this filthy act, and his even more insulting insinuation, her father had warned Pierre never to get near her again, or he would be shot.

He had been ordered to stay away from the fort.

She had not seen him for many months and was afraid that he had come today only to see her again, after having heard that she was there.

She watched him now with a guardedness as he laughed and jeered and continued to gamble with Shadow Bear and the other warriors. They all sat in a close circle a few feet from Shiona and Dancing Breeze, who had no idea how Shiona was feeling about the other white person in the village.

Dancing Breeze was sighing and enjoying some of the young braves who had their horses on parade.

Upon having first seen them herself Shiona had been in awe of how each youth had brushed his horse until it shone, and how they had placed wreaths of sweet grass around their necks and tied eagle feathers to their tails and manes.

But when Pierre had joined the gamblers, sitting beside Shadow Bear in the tight circle of players, her eyes stayed glued on the untrustworthy man, hoping that Shadow Bear would realize it if Pierre tried one of his sneaky tricks on him while gambling.

For now it all seemed fun and games for the gamblers as they played what she knew was their favorite game of chance. Although keeping an eye on Pierre, a tall and thin man who sported a narrow black mustache and goatee and wore an expensive suit today, with a gold-embroidered vest, Shiona also watched the game and how it was played.

Four mittens were laid down in a row.

A bullet was concealed beneath one of the mittens.

It was the business of the others who had not placed the mittens there to tell which mitten contained the bullet.

Of course, she knew that there was but one chance in four that the guesser would hit it right, but when one succeeded in finding the bullet, it was his turn to hide it.

The group of gamblers was large, but only one on each side was chosen to play this particular game at a time. The others watched the turns of fortune and sang a tune that was appropriate to this game, accompanied by the steady, rhythmic beats of a lone drum.

Shiona was surprised to see just how absorbed the men were in the game. They were so intent that they did not notice Silent Arrow and Moon Glow sneaking away from the crowd to be alone.

Suddenly Pierre leaped up from the ground, causing Shiona to flinch with alarm. She studied him, and saw how he glanced over at her, a leer on his face as he shouted that it was time to hear music besides that which was being played on a drum.

"I have brought my fiddle!" he announced, drawing all eyes to him. Even the gamblers stood and watched him. "Who would like to hear tunes played from my fiddle?"

Shiona could tell that these people had heard him play his fiddle before, because they all smiled and clapped in response to his question, which was all the encouragement he needed.

She had heard him play once, and that had been while she and her family had been at his villa. She had to admit that he was quite skilled, but she had no desire to hear him. She only prayed silently for his quick exit, for she was afraid that he might forget his place as well as what she was to this proud Lakota chief, for word had spread among the people of Shadow Bear's love for Shiona, and hers for him.

Luckily, she had not seen anyone openly disapprove of their relationship, but surely it was because everyone had heard that she had all but saved Silent Arrow's life by having tended to his wound while they were both in the cave that day.

Shiona watched Pierre unwrap the fiddle, then tensed as he made certain to walk closely past her as he made his way back to where everyone awaited the pleasure of his fiddle playing.

When Pierre was directly beside Shiona, he leaned low and spoke softly to her, so softly that even Dancing Breeze, who sat beside her, would not hear his insult. "Do you feel naughty today?" Pierre whispered, laughing softly at the blush that his words produced, then stepped away and began playing his fiddle. A young brave brought a flute that he had recently made and accompanied Pierre's music with that of his own, while everyone watched, entranced.

Shiona was fuming over how Pierre had so brazenly insulted her again. She couldn't believe how daring he was to have said that to her while among people who knew this was their chief's woman.

But, of course, Pierre had been clever enough to say what he had said loud enough for only Shiona to hear. The fact remained, though, what he had said would never be forgotten by her.

She hoped she was not visibly trembling as Shadow Bear gazed at her from where he stood with friends. She knew that Shadow Bear had no idea what had just transpired between her and a man she knew he trusted.

But when she turned her gaze back toward Pierre and saw a glitter in his deep blue eyes, she could not help but believe that he was mentally undressing her, as he had so often before her father had caught on to this man's filthy side.

Tired of him looking at her, Shiona rose quickly to her feet and went to Shadow Bear's tepee.

She had looked over her shoulder at Shadow Bear and had seen how he had started to follow her but was stopped by several children who surrounded him, questioning him about the music and how it came from the wooden box. She hurried inside the tepee, breathless from her anger and the insults brought on by the crazed Frenchman.

Yes, crazed, for what other man would dare come into a village of Lakota people whose chief was in love with the very woman the Frenchman insulted?

"He is quite stupid, that is for certain," Shiona murmured to herself, leaning to shove a log into the fire, for she was chilled through and through by the experience of moments ago.

When the fiddling stopped, Shiona stiffened. She knew that Pierre's horse and pack mule were not far from the tepee in which she had sought refuge from him. But surely he would not dare enter the chief's lodge without permission.

Shiona scarcely breathed as she listened for footsteps that she knew would be Pierre's as he came to his steeds. She doubled her hands into tight fists at her sides, softly praying that he would not be daft enough to come into the tepee, for she knew that he had seen her leave the crowd and had surely watched to see where she had gone.

"Please . . . oh please . . . ," she whispered as she gazed through the smoke hole overhead, seeking solace in prayer. But Shiona could not just stand there and wait to see what Pierre would do next.

She crept to the entrance flap, slowly slid it aside far enough for her to see through. She saw Pierre as he was standing beside his pack mule, placing his fiddle in its case, thankfully unaware that she was watching him. Suddenly a blanket that had been rolled up and tied at the other side of the mule came partially unrolled.

Shiona felt the color drain from her face when she saw several arrows all rolled into one inside the blanket. She grew faint when she realized that those arrows were exactly like the ones that had killed not only her father, brother, and mother, but also had wounded Silent Arrow.

Oh, Lord, she thought to herself, could

155

Pierre, not Indians, be the murderer?

She quickly dropped the flap when he looked her way, catching sight of her.

Her heart raced.

She was terribly afraid of him now.

And she had seen how fond Shadow Bear and his people were of him.

Surely they would not believe her over him, for it was apparent that they had known this man for much longer than they had known Shiona. He had never given them any cause to see him as anything but a close friend with whom they shared much fun and camaraderie. It would be her word against his.

She doubted they would look under the blanket even if she suggested it, for fear of insulting this man they were so fond of and who brought gifts that made the women's eyes widen with joy!

She had watched as he handed out coffee she now knew the Lakota called "black medicine," and how he had brought enough for everyone. He had even cleverly brought sugar for the coffee. Shiona had seen the Lakota asking for more and more sweet lumps, which he eagerly gave to them for their coffee. Yes, it was obvious that he had them all wrapped around his little finger, perhaps even Shadow Bear!

"Oh, Lord, what should I do?" Shiona whispered, wringing her hands before her. She knew that if she stayed there, she was a target. He knew she had seen his murder weapons.

No matter how much she loved Shadow Bear, Shiona saw now that she had no choice but to flee. Yes. She had no choice but to leave and find a way to begin a new life elsewhere.

But first . . . she must have the gold!

It was surely the one thing that could guarantee her a comfortable, safe future!

CHAPTER 16

... How fit to employ
All the heart and the soul
and the senses forever in joy!
                    — Robert Browning

Knowing that she had no other choice but to leave the Lakota village, and the only man she knew she would ever love, Shiona gathered up a few of her belongings and stuffed them into her travel bag. She gazed at the lovely Indian dress that she wore. She knew she shouldn't wear it away from the village because of what it might represent to the white world. But she also knew that she didn't have much time to make her exit. She wasn't sure just how much longer the Lakota celebration was going to last, and when it ended Shadow Bear would return to his lodge.

Tears rushed into her eyes to think that

she had just found happiness again after having recently lost so much in her life and she now had to walk away from it.

But first she had to escape from Pierre. He had definitely seen her looking from the tepee. Surely he knew that she had seen the proof that tied him to the murders and would know that she would tell Shadow Bear.

She knew he was guilty and she would, in time, make him pay for his crimes. Once she felt that she wasn't in danger of him finding her, she would go to a fort and turn in the murdering demon.

She would wait there until he was caught, and hopefully hung, and then be on her way, to seek love and happiness elsewhere. Once she left Shadow Bear's village, she would put him and memories of him from her mind.

She was once again alone in the world, and she would make it on her own.

Although tiny, she was headstrong and willful.

Yes, she would be all right.

She had no choice but to see that she was, for she, and her courage, was all that she had!

She packed her bag, and still wearing the lovely dress, which she planned to change from in the hidden cave, she stepped up to the entrance flap. Breathless with fear, she slowly shoved the flap aside and peeked outside.

Pierre had rejoined the celebration and was talking with Shadow Bear.

Shiona looked through her tears at Shadow Bear, her heart aching. His camaraderie with Pierre was evident.

Shiona knew that if she didn't flee at this moment, while all eyes were elsewhere, she might never have another opportunity. With all the haste she could manage, she fled from the tepee.

She knew that even the sentries had left their posts to join the fun, for as far as the Lakota knew, they were in no imminent danger from anyone.

When she reached the back side of the village, she stopped and sucked in a wild breath of air. She waited a moment to see if someone had followed her, foiling her plan. But when no one came and she heard the laughter and music behind her, she knew that thus far she was home free.

Shiona hurried toward the corral, found her horse, and mounted, balancing her bag in front of her. Riding bareback, she guided the horse quickly into the dark, dank shadows of the forest behind the village. She wove her steed in and out of the way of tall trees, then soon found herself riding across a wide stretch of land in the direction of the cave. The parched grass scattered beneath the pounding of her steed's hooves, sending it airborne and making her sneeze, but she continued onward.

She must get to the cave as quickly as possible. She hoped to retrieve the gold and leave again before she was missed at the village. Then she would find her way to the nearest fort, where she would ask for momentary protection, and if she couldn't find a fort, she would find someone who would hear her story and offer her help and safety. Once her story about Pierre was revealed, and someone believed her, the cavalry could take charge and find him.

She coughed and wiped at her eyes as the black ash continued to fly up and onto her face. She needed to stop for a drink, and to wipe her eyes and face clean of the ash, but she didn't have time. She must arrive at the cave, get the gold, then flee again.

Finally she reached the cave. She drew a tight rein, dismounted, and led her steed inside to keep it hidden until she was ready to leave.

She looked guardedly around her, shuddering at how everything was so dark and dreary. She gazed at the burned-out ashes of the fire that she had built herself upon first arriving there with her brother. Pangs of loneliness for her brother made her heart ache.

Desperately wanting to get this over, Shiona reached down for some matches that she had left there earlier and shoved several into the pocket of her dress, then lit one and began making her way to the back of the cave, where her father had hidden the gold.

"I'll get through this," she whispered as she penetrated the darkest recesses of the cave. "Lord, oh Lord, please let me live to see another day."

CHAPTER 17

Love's wing moults when caged and cap-
    tured,
Only free he soars enraptured.
                            — Thomas Campbell

Dusk fell in a gray shadow over the village. Up until now Shadow Bear's time had been fully occupied, and he only now realized that Shiona was no longer in sight. That had to mean that she had grown tired and returned to his tepee.

It had been quite a long day, with all sorts of excitement among his people, and with much food that even now filled the air with its tantalizing aroma. He assumed that his grandmother had also returned to her own tepee after having tended to the children of this village who loved and admired her.

A woman of good heart, she had given of her time willingly, and her time with the

163

children seemed to ease her grief after the death of her husband.

He wondered if he should go and check on her first? Of late she had looked so much more tired and weary and he had not seen her touch much food, although he had seen one woman after another offer her trays of refreshment.

Ho, yes. His grandmother should come before Shiona, for Shiona was strong despite her recent fever.

Although she was tiny, when he embraced her, he had felt muscle in her body. A woman of muscle was to be admired, for it proved she had endurance, which women needed for the work that Lakota women performed each day in order to make a happy home for their loved ones.

As he walked toward his grandmother's tepee, several young braves ran up to him, stopping him.

"My chief, today was a great day," one of the children, whose name was Quick Fox said. "Did you see our foot race? Did you see this brave win that race?"

Growing more anxious by the minute to check on his grandmother so that he could go to Shiona, Shadow Bear fought to check his impatience. These were his people's children, which made them also his. Besides,

Shadow Bear adored children.

He placed a gentle hand on Quick Fox's bare shoulder. "*Ho,* I saw the race and saw who was the victor," he said, smiling. "Did not your mother give you a name that matched your abilities of running?"

Quick Fox's eyes widened. "But, my chief, I could not run on the day of my birth, so how would my mother know to call me a name that matched my abilities as a runner when I was older?" he asked innocently.

"She saw you, in her mind's eye, as an older child, and when she did see you, she saw you as a runner," Shadow Bear patiently explained.

As he looked past the children who stood now in a half circle around him, and he again looked for Shiona, who might now be in view, and he still did not see her, he could not help but feel a strange pang of concern.

As he thought back to earlier, when he had introduced Pierre to Shiona, he knew without them telling him, that they knew each other.

The look in Shiona's eyes was that of contempt.

The look in Pierre's eyes was one of desire.

It was after that, when Shiona left them, to go and sit with some women, that he had lost track of her.

A laugh from the children brought Shadow Bear's mind back to the present. He laughed softly as he moved his hand from Quick Fox's shoulder and placed it on another child's.

"I must see to my grandmother's welfare," he said.

The children nodded, then ran off, each one seeming to speak at the same time as they chattered about the foot race again, saying that tomorrow they would race on their ponies.

Shadow Bear stepped gingerly into his grandmother's tepee. He found her asleep beside her slow-burning fire, a blanket snug around her.

The fire's glow sent dancing shadows onto his grandmother's old face, causing a sadness to sweep through Shadow Bear. He knew that he did not have that much more time with her. Her husband was beckoning her from the other side to join him, so that they could walk together through fields of sunflowers again, with buffalo nearby. For all of his people believed that when one died, he went to a better place than what he had left behind.

He stayed long enough to place some wood on his grandmother's fire and to place a gentle kiss on her leathery cheek. "I will return when you are awake," he whispered.

"I am awake," Dancing Breeze suddenly said, her old eyes opening. She smiled. "I was only resting my eyes."

"Did you overtire yourself by being at the celebration for too long?" Shadow Bear asked.

He knelt beside her and placed a gentle hand on her face.

"Somewhat," Dancing Breeze murmured; then she took his hand and held it. "I came to my lodge and slept awhile."

"That is good," Shadow Bear said. "You should always take time to rest, no matter what else might be happening in our village."

"Grandson, while I slept, I saw a vision," Dancing Breeze said, a seriousness now in her eyes. She gently squeezed his hand.

"A vision?" Shadow Bear said, forking an eyebrow. "What did you see?"

"Wolves," Dancing Breeze said. "I saw not only one wolf, but four."

"What is the meaning behind this vision of wolves?" Shadow Bear asked.

"You were also in the vision. The wolves were a threat to your safety." She clung harder to his hand. "Grandson, beware of wolves when you are away from the village," she entreated.

"Is that all you saw?" Shadow Bear asked. "You did not see what the wolves were doing?"

"They were threatening you," she said, her voice cracking with emotion.

She took her hand from his and closed her eyes. "I must rest some more." She opened her eyes again and gazed directly into his. "But beware of wolves."

"*Ho,* yes, I will," he said. "I will return soon and sit with you. We can talk."

She nodded softly, then sighed as she drifted off.

Shadow Bear gazed at her a moment longer, full of wonder about her latest vision. He spun around and left the lodge, and with eagerness in his steps, he hurried to his own.

When he first stepped inside he was alarmed, for both Shiona and her travel bag were missing.

If she was gone, did that mean that she had fled? Had she cared for him at all?

Was she an *ikomi,* trickster, like those that were the center of so many nighttime stories told around the fires? Had she only pretended to care for him in order to gain his trust so that she was free to come and go?

His stomach clenched as her betrayal sank in. He raced to the corral, only to learn that

Shiona's horse was also gone.

Feeling deceived and foolish, Shadow Bear hurried back inside his tepee and attached his sheathed knife to his waist.

He also grabbed his rifle.

He did not plan to use these things on the lying woman, but he did plan to travel as far as it took to find her, even if it took him into enemy territory!

He would not stop until he found her!

He went back to the corral, saddled his horse, Star, slid his rifle into the gun boot at the side of his steed; then, without telling anyone that he was leaving, he mounted and rode away.

There was still enough light to see the footprints in the black ash as he reached that part of the ground where the flames had not been stopped by the trench dug by his people.

Ho, yes, he saw a horse's prints in the black ash, and he knew it was her steed's prints, for they were freshly made.

He rode onward, his eyes never leaving the prints in the ash, his heart sick with betrayal. He tried not to think of how it was to look into her beautiful violet eyes, or how his fingertips felt as he ran his hands through the softness of her golden hair.

And, ah, when he had held her and kissed

169

her, had it not been pure heaven?

"How could I have allowed her to come so easily into my life and heart?" he shouted at the sky as he looked heavenward and saw the moon taking the place of the sun as darkness now fell all across Lakota land.

He doubled a hand into a fist and shook it toward the heavens. "Fool!" he cried. "*Ina,* Mother! *Ahte,* Father! Do you not now see your son as a fool?" His jaw tight, he gazed down at the ground. He was no longer able to make out the tracks, but he knew where Shiona was surely headed.

The cave.

It was in the exact direction of her flight!

"What draws her there?" he whispered to himself, his eyebrows arching.

But he knew what drew him there with a heavy heart: a heart of fury.

"*Ikomi,* trickster!" he shouted, flinching when his voice echoed all around him, like many more voices in the night.

CHAPTER 18

A day of days! I let it come and go
As traceless as a thaw of bygone snow.
                    — Christina Rossetti

Having run out of matches, everything was
now like a black hole around her. Shiona
was determined, however, to find the gold
her father had left. She needed to find it
and get out of the area as quickly as possible.

She had found too many heartaches there.

Tears filled her eyes. She had found a man
she loved, only to learn that he was not the
sort of man she thought he was.

Anyone who allied himself with the sort
of man Pierre was, was surely of question-
able character himself. She wondered what
they did beyond the village.

What sort of schemes did they carry out
together?

She had no idea how she had thought an Indian could be trusted.

Had not she always been told that they couldn't?

But the way Shadow Bear had held her!

The way he had treated her, ever so gently!

How could she not believe he was anything but wonderful.

Knowing that she had to stop thinking about him and get on with her life, Shiona continued feeling her way along the wall of the cave, wincing when she felt the wet and soggy moss that grew there. Her fingers sought a slight slant to the rock wall. According to her father, this would lead her to a crack and then a deep indentation where the sack would be found.

She knew that her brother lay in the ground only a few footsteps away. The sadness of his loss ate away at her gut all over again, for at this moment she missed him so much, she thought she might die!

Maybe she would be better off in the ground with him, she thought bitterly to herself. Was there anyone in this wide world she could trust? Was there someone in this world who might truly love her and take her away from this loneliness that was overwhelming her?

With an enormous effort, Shiona pushed

those thoughts aside and continued her search. She ignored the ache in her fingers as she continued to run her hands over the rough surface of the cave wall. Suddenly she felt something brush against her arm.

Gasping with horror she yanked her hand back.

Oh, Lord, surely not!

Surely she had not felt an arm!

But when she heard the scratch and saw the sudden flare of a match, and then another, she took a shaky step backward. She found herself staring at a scarred, raw face of burns, and clothes ragged and black with ash. The man held a match in both hands, its feeble light allowing her to see him at least for a brief moment.

She knew now who it was!

She would never forget the strange green eyes contrasting against the copper skin, and even through the tangle of burned hair, she saw its brilliant, scarlet color.

"Jack Thunder Horse," she gasped, placing a hand to her throat.

Yes, she knew this man very well.

He had been the half-breed scout at Fort Chance.

Suddenly he used what remained of the two burning matches to set off what was left of the matches in the small box that he took from his front shirt pocket. He placed this makeshift lamp on a ledge of rock.

He then grabbed a knife from its sheath at his right side and held it out for Shiona to see. The small, sputtering flames from the matches glowed in the blade of the knife. Shiona scarcely breathed as she gazed at it. She was afraid that he would be using it on her very soon, but wondered why he saw her as a threat. Surely he saw that she had no weapon. It was only herself and her fear . . . and her hopelessness.

He reached his other hand to another small ledge of rock and grabbed what Shiona knew must be her father's bag of gold. "Were you coming in here to look for this?" Jack Thunder Horse asked, chuckling beneath his breath. "Your father had no idea I watched his every move. I knew where he got the gold, how, and where he hid it. I would've come sooner, but the fire got in the way." He laughed throatily. "It changed my looks to something pretty, don't you think?"

Still Shiona said nothing. She was too stunned and afraid to speak. Her knees were rubbery weak from fear and her heart was pounding so hard now, she felt as though it might leap from inside her chest.

"There ain't much light left in those

matches, pretty thing, so tell me now where that map is," Jack Thunder Horse said.

He stepped closer to her.

He teasingly swung the bag of gold up before her eyes. "Thought this would be yours, didn't you?" he taunted. "When your papa died, you thought you were going to be a rich pretty thing, didn't you? Why, you and your brother might have even been the ones to kill your pa so that you could have your hands on his gold."

"What a disgusting thing to say," Shiona said, her anger finally giving her fuel to speak. "You probably killed him. You are nothing but —"

"Hush up," Jack Thunder Horse said, glowering at her. "Like I said. We're runnin' out of time. Where did your papa plant that map? I want all of the gold, not only a small portion."

Then he stepped even closer to her. "Or better yet, little angel, maybe we can share what we pan from now on," he said menacingly. "We'd both be rich. And wouldn't we make quite a pair when we build us a fine and pretty home? A lovely golden-haired lady a wife to a half-breed whose face is hideously scarred for life."

Shiona shuddered at the thought of what he was suggesting. "I have no idea where the map is, and I abhor you, so how could you possibly imagine me sharing anything with the likes of you?" she said, visibly shuddering.

"Well, I saw no harm in suggesting it," Jack Thunder Horse said, shrugging. "Now don't tell me that I've gotten all burned and disfigured for nothing. Damn it, Shiona, tell me where that map is." He leered at her.

"And reconsider about being my partner," he said. "Tell me where the map is and we can be partners. I've always enjoyed looking at you, but had to look from afar since your pa was always there ready to kill any man who was interested in you. You can't imagine how often I hungered to feel your breasts. Now I can. There ain't nothin' much you can do about it. I've got the weapon. You don't. Now tell me, pretty thing, wouldn't you enjoy havin' a half-breed lover?"

Shiona's mind was spinning.

What could she do?

If she didn't cooperate with him, wouldn't he eventually decide that the one bag of gold was enough and slit her throat and leave her there, dead, with her brother?

When the matches suddenly burned out, Shiona took advantage of it. She reached out and gave Jack Thunder Horse a hard shove, then bolted toward the cave entrance, hoping and praying that she could get there before Jack Thunder Horse got his bearings and caught up with her.

But she could hear the crunch of rock behind her as well as him cursing. She knew he was gaining on her.

"Ska-winohinca!" he shouted in his Indian tongue. "Bad woman! Stop! If you don't, when I catch up with you, I won't do any more talking. I'll kill you, instead."

Knowing that was true, Shiona raced ahead. She breathed a sigh of relief and thanked the good Lord above when she finally reached the cave opening and was able to flee it into the night.

She didn't get far before she stopped, stunned, when, by the light of the moon, she saw Shadow Bear just ahead of her.

Then she heard Jack Thunder Horse's voice behind her, cursing and calling her name. Fear squeezed her heart, and she ran to Shadow Bear, sobbing.

Having heard Jack Thunder Horse's voice, Shadow Bear grabbed Shiona into his arms protectively just as the half-breed burst out of the cave, momentarily stunned when he saw Shadow Bear there with Shiona.

For a moment Shadow Bear and Jack Thunder Horse glared at each other. Years ago, the two had been allies, but when Jack

Thunder Horse became the white man's scout, the two had become enemies.

Suddenly Jack Thunder Horse ran past Shadow Bear and Shiona, accidentally dropping the bag in the process. The gold spilled from the bag, glittering beneath the shine of the moon.

Shiona and Shadow Bear broke apart as they heard a horse thundering away into the darkness as the half-breed fled.

Safe from that scarred, evil man, Shiona again flung herself into Shadow Bear's arms, surprised when he stiffened and didn't return her hug.

She stepped slowly away and gazed into his eyes, the moon's glow revealing mistrust in their depths.

Shadow Bear looked down at the gold, realizing that it had a role in what was happening tonight, for did it not make white people do strange things?

"Why did you leave the village?" Shadow Bear blurted out. "Was all that you said about your love for me nontruths? Did I not treat you well? Did not my people, especially my grandmother and brother, treat you well and with much compassion and love? Why would you leave a place of safety . . . of love? Was it the gold rocks that are on the ground close to your feet that made you flee my home . . . my love?"

He paused.

Then he spoke again, this time with even more intensity of feelings. "Tell me, Shiona. Was it the gold rocks that make white people go crazy with the need of it? Do you want those rocks more than the man who could protect and love you for eternity? In your culture, it is apparent that you were not taught that riches bring no man power or happiness."

He bent down and swept the gold back into the buckskin bag, then stood again and held it out toward her. "Prove to me which is more important," he said. "The rocks? Or a life with Shadow Bear?"

And even before she could respond to his question, she gasped when he slowly spilled the gold at Shiona's feet.

She stared down at the pile of gold as the moon cast its white sheen onto it. She did know the wealth that lay at her feet . . . what it could truly do for her.

Yet hadn't her father died because of it?

In a sense hadn't it caused her brother's death, because surely Seth would not have been ambushed near the cave were it not for that damnable gold.

Yes, damnable.

In truth, she now knew that she hated it

and felt guilty for having thought for one minute that it could give her what she wanted in life, when in truth all she wanted was the man who stood so near she could smell the wondrous outdoor aroma of his flesh.

Yet she had fled Shadow Bear for more reasons than the gold.

She was torn now with what she should do.

Trust him?

Or take the gold and start a new life as she had planned to do.

CHAPTER 19

Love's a fire that needs renewal
Of fresh beauty for its fuel.
— Thomas Campbell

"You are too quiet," Shadow Bear said, breaking the silence between them. "I can only believe that you have made your choice. I will leave you now, but before I go, I want to wish you well on your road of life. I do know the riches that lay at your feet and how such rocks have lured people to their deaths. I just regret that it has had an effect on you that might lead to your own demise."

He so badly wished to reach for Shiona and hold her one last time, for already he ached inside from missing her.

But he had pride.

He would not allow it to be taken from him by a woman who chose rocks over him, no matter what they could give her.

More often than not, once white people had gold nuggets in their pockets, they did not gain anything from them other than pure misery.

He started to turn, but stopped and stared when he saw Shiona suddenly stamp a foot on the gold, grinding it into the ash until it was no longer in sight.

Her pulse racing, her violet eyes now locked with Shadow Bear's, Shiona stepped closer to him and placed a gentle hand on his cheek. "I want nothing to do with the gold," she declared. "It has already cost me too much. My family . . ."

"If that is so, why then did you come for it, for is not that the reason you fled me and my people?" he said, the flesh of her palm against his own flesh sending a message of wonder to his heart.

"No, Shadow Bear, I did not leave you, your people, nor your village, for the gold," Shiona said, searching his eyes, so badly wanting to see forgiveness and understanding in them. "I saw that I had no choice but to leave."

"I do not understand," Shadow Bear said gravely.

He reached and took her other hand, holding both now with desperation, for if he let go of her hands, he was afraid that he might be letting go of her forever.

"Shadow Bear, I fled a white man who was at your village, only then to encounter another man here at the cave. Jack Thunder Horse knew my father had hidden a bag of gold here." She swallowed hard and lowered her eyes momentarily.

"But Jack Thunder Horse wanted more than the gold he had already found," she said, her voice breaking. "He wanted a map that would lead to much more gold . . . a map that my father had drawn that showed where more gold could be found."

"I know of that man Jack Thunder Horse, but what puzzles me is who else you spoke of tonight," Shadow Bear said, his voice drawn. "What other man are you referring to? Who was at my village who frightened you so much that you felt you had no choice but to run from him?"

Then his eyes widened when he thought of Pierre DuSault. He was the only white man who had been at his village tonight!

"Pierre DuSault," he said, watching her reaction. "He was at my village tonight. He is white. Is he the one you fled from?"

Shiona nodded, then, in a rush of words, told him about having seen the wrapped arrows on Pierre's mule.

"So don't you see?" Shiona said, watching

his reaction to all that was being revealed to him. "The arrows I saw in Pierre's possession had the same drawing on them as those that killed my loved ones and injured Silent Arrow."

Shadow Bear slowly dropped her hands, then turned away from her, his mind aswirl. He had never seen a mean side to Pierre. He was arrogant, a trait he had seen in most white men, but he had seen nothing that would indicate that Pierre was capable of murder and deceit.

He turned again to face Shiona and gazed intently into her eyes. "Why?" he said thickly. "Why would he kill your father and the others of your family? And why would he harm my brother? Our relations are amiable."

"But think about it, Shadow Bear. Did you not notice how Silent Arrow left the ceremony with Moon Glow almost immediately when Pierre arrived? The celebration was for your brother, yet he felt a need to abandon it. Don't you see? He would only do this because he didn't want to be where Pierre was. Surely something happened between them before Pierre chose to try to kill him."

"But what could that be?" Shadow Bear

said, kneading his brow thoughtfully. "Why?"

"All for the sake of gold," Shiona said softly. "Surely Pierre was tracking my father all along, after having received word from someone that my father had discovered gold. He must have known about the cave where my father hid the gold. He planned to silence everyone who also knew, or who were close to knowing."

"But Silent Arrow? He was not a man who would be lured by the shine of gold. He knows of its evil, the same as I know of it. He would never allow himself to become involved in such a thing that could bring only heartbreak to his people."

"Silent Arrow must have posed a threat to Pierre, somehow. He may have thought that Silent Arrow knew about the gold, or would soon know, whereas your brother was only seeking shelter from the fire."

She paused, then said, "Your brother just happened to be at the wrong place at the wrong time."

She thought of that day when her brother was killed. Surely the only reason she had been spared was because Pierre hoped that after all of her family was gone, she would lean on him for support when he offered it.

He had not counted on Shadow Bear

entering the picture, or the fire that delayed his final plans.

She would never forget the look on his face when Pierre arrived at the village and saw her there. At that very moment, he must have begun forming another plot, a way to take her from the Lakota village, get her to his villa, and keep her there, hidden from the world.

A shiver suddenly raced up and down her spine when she realized that Pierre might even now be planning Shadow Bear's demise, since Shadow Bear now had a role in Shiona's life, and not just any role.

Surely Pierre had put two and two together after he had seen Shiona at the village dressed as one of their maidens.

"Shadow Bear, we should get out of here," she said, grabbing him by an arm. "Quickly. I feel as though we are being watched."

A soft hooting came through the night air, ghostly in its sound, and when Shiona looked around and saw two glittering eyes in the dark, she gasped.

"It is only an owl's eyes that you see," Shadow Bear said, chuckling beneath his breath. "It is good that the owl survived the fire, as most birds and animals did not."

"An owl?" Shiona said, sighing, then laughed softly. "Thank goodness."

Her smile faded. "But I still feel that we should return to your village," she said, swallowing hard. "We are so vulnerable out here alone. Should Jack Thunder Horse decide to, he could circle around and sneak up on us and kill us both before we knew it was he who did it."

Shadow Bear placed his hands at her waist and drew her close to him. Their eyes met and held in the moonlight, and then everything but Shadow Bear was nonexistent as his lips came down onto hers in a wondrous kiss.

She twined her arms around his neck and returned the kiss, her body against his seeming so right and wonderful.

But Shadow Bear did see the danger in being there, so he stepped away from her, took her hand, and led her to her steed.

When he saw that she had not taken the time to saddle the horse, he took her to his own horse and lifted her into the saddle, knowing she would be much more comfortable than being made to ride bareback on her steed.

"Thank you," she murmured, understanding why he had placed her on his horse instead of hers. She laughed softly. "It was quite uncomfortable riding that way."

"From this day forth, I will make all things

good and right for you," Shadow Bear said, handing her the reins. "Whatever you want, all you need is to ask. You will then have it."

"I was so wrong to leave you," she said, her voice breaking. "I never shall again. I promise."

"I will make it so that you will not want to leave," Shadow Bear said, then turned and mounted her horse.

Shadow Bear rode up next to her. "My *mitawin,* woman, let us go home," he said.

"Yes, let's," Shiona replied, loving the sound of the word "home."

As they rode off together, the ash swirling at their horse's hooves, Shiona looked over her shoulder where she had smashed the gold into the ash, and then up at the cave.

She looked quickly away, then looked over her shoulder once again, but this time only to say a final good-bye to her beloved brother, for she didn't plan to come to this cave ever again.

The map could rot there for all she cared.

She felt the sting of tears in her eyes when she recalled something her father had always said about things that he saw as worthless. As he would discard this or that item, he would always say, "Good riddance of bad rubbish." That was exactly how Shiona felt about the map and the gold!

CHAPTER 20

But our love it was stronger by far than
   the love
Of those who were older than we.
             — Edgar Allan Poe

Shiona could hardly believe how things had changed since yesterday. She was back with Shadow Bear after having almost lost him, and she couldn't be happier. They had arrived at the village after midnight, and exhausted, had fallen asleep in each other's arms. They had awakened before anyone else, and had gone to the river to bathe, returning fresh and clean to Shadow Bear's tepee.

Later, when everyone was awake, two groups of warriors would ride from the village. One group would go and search for Jack Thunder Horse, and the other would bring Pierre DuSault back to the Lakota village for questioning.

But for now, it was only Shiona and Shadow Bear.

Both were undressed.

She was sitting beside the fire on plush pelts.

After securing the entranceway ties, Shadow Bear turned and gazed at Shiona with burning eyes, a trail of fire left by the touch of his eyes on her skin. Shiona shot him a look of shyness through her thick lashes, for she knew what would soon transpire. She would know the true meaning of being a woman, for she would be making love with a man for the first time in her life!

Without saying anything Shadow Bear knelt before her. "You are certain about what we are going to do?" he asked seriously. He reached out and placed a gentle hand on her cheek. "Or would you rather wait until later? I want you to feel as much as I, while making love."

"This is all so new to me," Shiona said, feeling the heat of a blush rush to her cheeks. "But, yes, I am here because I want to be, and yes, I would like to make love with you," she said softly. "My heart aches for you. My body cries out for you."

She reached up and took his hand from

her cheek, then placed it just above her breast, the nearness of his hand causing her heart to skip a wondrous beat.

Shadow Bear didn't have to hear her say any more. He watched her eyes as he slid his hand down and cupped her breast, the softness of her flesh against his causing the heat to build within his loins.

"I will be gentle," he said huskily. "The first time a woman makes love there is some pain, but the pain does not last long. You then forevermore will receive only pleasure as our bodies come together in a love dance."

Shiona was keenly aware of the sensual awakening of her body, a sexual excitement building the more he looked at her and touched her.

"Just love me," she murmured, trying not to think about the pain that he had mentioned.

Shadow Bear swept his arms around her, and with his body, pressed her gently down onto the pelts.

With a sob, Shiona clung to him when she felt that part of him that she knew would pleasure her start probing where a feathering of golden hair lay at the juncture of her thighs.

"I shall kiss the pain away," Shadow Bear

whispered against her lips, and as he kissed her, he shoved his manhood inside her, past that thin strip of flesh that proved she was a virgin, then farther still inside her and began his eager thrusts.

He rained kisses on her closed eyes and on her hair, then captured her lips beneath his as his thrusts continued and she now began to move her body with his.

He wrapped his arms around her and drew her body even more closely to his. She sought his mouth with a wildness and desperation, knowing now that she was way past the moment of pain, and that she was enjoying this newness that brought her such pleasure. Shadow Bear drove into her more swiftly and surely, his breathing ragged, that hollow ache within him before he had met Shiona drifting away, being replaced by a singing and soaring of their joined flesh.

"I have waited for you all of my life," Shadow Bear groaned against her lips. "I shall never let you go."

"I am not going anywhere," Shiona whispered. "You are all I want."

With a fierceness, he held her even more closely to his hard body, pressing himself against her as ecstasy peaked with bone-weakening intensity.

Breathless, her body a river of sensations,

Shiona clung to him, now realizing what her body had been yearning for these last years as she had grown into a mature woman.

"I am almost frantic with a passion I never knew existed," Shadow Bear sighed into her ear as he felt the urgency building within him. "Do you feel the same?"

"I feel the same, and surely, oh, surely so much more," Shiona said, her voice sounding foreign to herself in its strange huskiness.

"Now is the time," Shadow Bear said, pausing momentarily to devour her with his eyes. "You are about to realize the most wondrous of feelings a man and woman can bring to each other."

Her heart pounding, her head reeling from the pleasure that she felt within her already, she swallowed hard, gazed back at him, then closed her eyes and became lost in total ecstasy as he thrust once, twice, and three times, and everything within her seemed to explode in many sparkling colors as she felt a pleasure that she found hard to believe existed!

Their bodies rocked and quaked as they both found the exquisite sensations they had sought, and even when those feelings passed, their bodies still strained together hungrily.

"What we did . . . ," Shiona whispered against his cheek as he still lay above her, his arms so wonderful and strong around her, her thoughts lazy with pleasure. "It was as though pure lightning had shot through me."

She watched him as he rolled away from her and stretched out on his back beside her. She then turned to him and softly caressed his brow. "Was it the same for you?" she murmured.

He smiled lazily at her, then took her hand and held it. "That and more," he said, chuckling when he saw her eyes widen.

"How could you have felt more than I?" she asked. "It was as though I entered some sort of paradise."

She trembled with sensations new to her as he slowly swept his hand down her body.

"You will see," he said, chuckling. "You will see how each time we make love you will find new, wonderful sensations that will war with how you have already felt."

"I have much to look forward to, then," Shiona said, welcoming a blanket when he drew one over them.

"You do have much to learn, but not all sexually," Shadow Bear said. He reached for one of her hands as the fire burned softly in the fire pit. "As one of my people, you will learn that every day begins with a salute to the sun, and as a bringer of light, it is recognized whether its face is visible or whether it is hidden by a clouded sky."

"But I have not heard you address the sun or salute it," Shiona said.

"That is because there is no kneeling, no words spoken, nor hands raised, but in every Lakota heart there is just a thought of tribute," Shadow Bear proudly explained.

He turned to her so that their eyes met. "You will learn that no assembly of our people is required for that tribute, either. Each and every person, on his own account, holds his own moment of worship."

He nodded toward the closed entrance flap. "Outside, you will notice that further recognition is given the sun by the erection of the Lakota village with every tepee door facing the east," he said.

"Do your people actually worship the sun?" Shiona asked, eager to learn about Shadow Bear's customs, for she was going to be his wife and needed to know all things Lakota as quickly as possible in order to please his people.

"No, we do not actually worship the sun," Shadow Bear said softly. "We merely recognize the bearing it has upon all life, mani-

195

festing as it does the universal powers of the Great Mystery. When the Lakota pray or sing songs of praise, the sun carries them directly to *Wakan-Tanka*."

The blanket falling away from her, Shiona moved to her knees and studied Shadow Bear as he, too, sat up. "Do you believe that I can truly learn everything that is necessary for me to be a proud chief's wife?" she blurted out.

"You already know much," Shadow Bear said, standing. He grabbed his breechclout and put it on, then slid his feet into moccasins. Then he reached a hand down for Shiona. "Get dressed. I have someplace to take you this morning."

"You do?" Shiona asked, reaching for the dress that she had worn yesterday. Although it had splashes of ash on it, she didn't think it was right to wear her ordinary clothes now, since she was soon to be a proud Lakota chief's bride.

She also knew that there was hardly any other way to look Lakota, for her hair was golden, while theirs was black, their skin was copper, and hers was white.

The only difference could be made in her attire and she hoped to have more dresses soon, so that she could always look fresh and clean for her husband each morning.

"Where are you taking me?" she asked, combing her fingers through her thick hair, hoping to release as many tangles as she could before getting a chance to brush it.

"Just come and see," Shadow Bear said, his eyes twinkling as he held a hand out for her after untying the ties at the entrance-way.

She eagerly walked from the tepee with him, blushing when the women who were outside the lodge working on pelts or preparing food for the noon meal saw her leave their chief's lodge, wondering if they saw a difference in her.

She felt different now after having made love. She felt like a true woman for the first time in her life.

She smiled at those whose eyes lingered on her, then turned from them and walked ahead with Shadow Bear. She noted the warriors gathering at the larger corral, knowing why they had come.

They were waiting for their chief to join them on the hunt for the two men.

She hoped Pierre would not be that hard to find, but if he suspected anything was wrong, he might have fled, just as Jack Thunder Horse had disappeared.

"Shouldn't you go and join your war-riors?" Shiona asked, drawing Shadow

Bear's eyes to her.

"They await their chief, no matter how long it takes," he said matter-of-factly. "My first duty of this morning is to my future wife, as is my second duty to you."

They continued walking past the tepees, the sun warm overhead, the breeze still somewhat spoiled with the smell of ash that lingered despite another sweet rain that had come through during the night.

When he stopped before a newly erected, clean white tepee, with pretty designs painted on the outside, she gave him a look of wonder.

"This is your lodge," Shadow Bear said, gesturing toward it. "Until we speak vows, you will have this lodge as your own, as I will have my own."

She questioned him with her eyes.

"It is best this way," Shadow Bear said huskily. "You need your own lodge for preparation of your marriage to me. And once we are man and wife, you will return again to live in my lodge with me. That is the way it is in my Lakota world."

"I see," Shiona murmured, studying the drawings on the new white tepee.

"A bright painted lodge, fine blankets, stacks of beadwork and plush robes and food speak of good living," he said, taking her by an elbow, ushering her inside the tepee. "This is all yours."

Shiona's breath was stolen away when she saw the many expensive plush pelts spread across the floor around the soft-burning fire in the fire pit.

Three beautifully beaded dresses were spread out on the far side of the lodge, as well as a shawl, moccasins, and yellow and blue ribbons, two of each.

Taken aback by all of these lovely things, Shiona could only beam with happiness at Shadow Bear.

"These are your possessions now," he explained. "And since you no longer have a family of your own, my people are your family."

"You are so generous," Shiona said, tears spilling from her eyes.

"You deserve all that is good on this earth," Shadow Bear said, drawing her into his embrace. "My woman . . . my wife . . . will never want for anything."

"Who would want any more than I already have?" Shiona murmured, gazing into his eyes. "I already have the world since I have you."

He lowered his lips to hers and gave her a soft, wondrous kiss, but was pulled away quickly when he heard the neighing of horses and knew that those who were saddled and ready for travel were getting restless.

"I must go now," he said. He gently framed her face between his hands. "But I will find it hard to wait until tonight when we will be together again."

"So shall I," Shiona responded as they walked hand in hand to the entrance flap.

Before he opened it, he drew her into his arms again and gave her a kiss, one that he hoped would sustain her until they came together again tonight around her lodge fire.

"I will miss being in your lodge," Shiona said as she moved slowly away from him.

"You do not need to, for I will be in yours each night until we come together as man and wife," he said, his eyes twinkling as he opened the entrance flap. "Moon Glow will be here soon to give you something to do as you await my return. You will enjoy what she brings for you."

"What is it?" she asked, following him from the tepee.

"You always have shown your admiration of the beadwork of my people," he said. "You will learn the art of beadwork today."

"Oh, that will be so wonderful," Shiona said, clasping her hands together before her.

Then her smile faded. She reached a hand

out for him. "Be careful," she said, melting inside when he took her hand for a moment while their eyes met and spoke volumes to each other, which they did not dare say aloud while the warriors looked toward them.

Then he rushed away from her and mounted his steed that Two Leaves had readied for him.

Shadow Bear turned and gave Shiona a nod and smile, then rode away.

A tremor flowed through Shiona's body, for she did not like thinking of where he was going.

She knew that Jack Thunder Horse was capable of out-and-out murder, but she wasn't sure of what Pierre DuSault might do in order to try and save his good name among the Lakota people.

"You will get yours, if not today, later," she vowed as she pictured Pierre in her mind's eye.

CHAPTER 21

Let us possess one world; each hath one,
and is one.

— John Donne

Shiona rode beside Shadow Bear on her
steed. She quickly looked heavenward as
her horse began neighing and shaking its
mane when a red-winged hawk, called a
sunhawk, suddenly appeared and circled
overhead. As it swept down from the sky,
shadowing everything below it with its
widespread, powerful wings, and calling
peent peent, she could not stop watching
the soaring bird.

It then flew away, up into the sky, where
several other sunhawks came together, soaring so beautifully it took Shiona's breath
away.

"I have never seen such a sight," she said,
sighing as she watched them fly farther away

until she could no longer see them. "And the way the one bird cried out so loud and clear, it was as though it was a warning of sorts."

"The sunhawk cries out its happiness today as it flies with its mate and friends," Shadow Bear said, having also watched the bird's flight. "The sunhawk is one of the 'winged peoples' and guardian spirit, given the ability of far vision and balance in all things. It is a spirit messenger, a reminder to man of his connectedness with the Great Spirit."

Once again Shiona was awed by this man who knew so much about so many creatures of nature.

"Are you enjoying our outing?" Shadow Bear asked as he sidled his horse more closely to hers as they traveled through fiddlehead ferns, a rock locust whirring by.

He was impressed by how lovely she was with her flushed cheeks, the sun warm on them this midmorning, and her golden hair flying loose in the wind behind her as she rode straight-backed in her saddle.

She wore a newly beaded dress and matching beaded moccasins, both gifts from Moon Glow. "Yes, I'm enjoying myself, although I can't put Jack Thunder Horse and Pierre from my mind," she confessed as she looked guardedly around her.

Yet her fear and suspicions seemed misplaced today while she was with Shadow Bear, riding where hawkweed and buttercups dotted the ground with a riot of color.

Their path was also bordered with birch and aspen, the nearby river almost beckoning with its unbroken shoreline. Yes, nature was all around her, this part of the land untouched by the fire that had recently devastated so much.

But things weren't always as they seemed. She just could not help but be afraid that either of those evil men might suddenly appear, stalking her and Shadow Bear. Both men seemed to have disappeared from the face of the earth. Shadow Bear's warriors had not found a trace of Jack Thunder Horse, and Pierre had also disappeared.

"It has been several days now since my warriors began searching for both Pierre and Jack Thunder Horse, and it has been decided that they both have fled the area, so do not concern yourself over them," Shadow Bear said.

His eyes narrowed with hate as he recalled how Pierre had made a fool of him and his people by feigning friendship, while all along he was a worthless, evil man.

"What did Pierre do to turn your father against him?" Shadow Bear asked.

"Father never confided in me about that," Shiona said, her voice drawn. "But a part of his reason was because he saw Pierre taking advantage of my innocence when he cornered me one day while no one was watching and . . . and . . . actually dared to touch my breast through my dress. After he left, I told my father. Father grew enraged over what Pierre did and said he would never again be welcome at the fort."

She lowered her eyes. "But it was not just that incident that caused my father to dislike Pierre," she continued. "He hinted at something being wrong between them, but never revealed what Pierre might have done besides humiliate me in such a way. It must have happened before the day he ordered Pierre away, for I had seen my father's attitude toward Pierre change at the dinner table earlier in the evening. He was cold and abrupt with Pierre. I smiled at that, for I saw how uncomfortable being treated in such a way made Pierre feel."

"I am sorry that he treated you wrongly. Had I known, I would not have invited him to our celebration. I would have never placed you in such an awkward position," Shadow Bear said, gazing intently into her eyes. "And it was because of him, and how you felt about my friendly relationship with him, that you left. I should have known something was terribly wrong by how you openly avoided that man."

"I'm sorry that I did not trust you," Shiona said, her voice catching. "But after seeing the arrows on Pierre's pack mule, and seeing the way you were so friendly with him, I could not help but think you had some sort of alliance with the man."

"Even after my brother was shot by one of those same designed arrows?" Shadow Bear asked, arching an eyebrow. His jaw tightened. "You should have told me immediately about those arrows. Had I known, I would have realized that I was wrongly allying myself with such a man as he."

"I know that now, and I truly apologize for running away like I did instead of coming to you," she said softly. "But what confuses me, now that I have had more time to think about it, is the fact that he could be so brazen as to bring the arrows among your people. He had to know that the design on the arrow would give him away should someone see them."

"Who is to say what makes a madman's mind work? Anyone who would heartlessly wander the land, killing and maiming the way he has surely done, is not a man of a clear, innocent mind," Shadow Bear said flatly. "And because my warriors could not find him, he will kill again."

"He fled that very night after the celebration. He had to know that I saw the arrows and would tell you about them. He did not know that I, instead, fled. So maybe he will be too afraid to kill again," Shiona suggested.

"And as far as Jack Thunder Horse is concerned, he knows better than to ever show his face again on Lakota land, for he knows the price he will pay for his evil ways," Shadow Bear said tightly. "But enough talk about those two evil men. It is a time for just the two of us. I wanted to check on how the land is faring since the fire, and then we can concentrate on our marriage. I am relieved that this part of the land was not affected, and where the ash does lie elsewhere, new sprouts are pushing their way through the blackness. More rains will wash away all of the ash and give nourishment to those plants, proving that nothing will stop them, not even a vicious fire."

"It is so beautiful here," Shiona said, sighing as she gazed slowly around her. "I am so glad the fire didn't reach this far. Just look at all of the varieties of flowers. And look at those bushes that are heavy with berries. Why, I see masses of pink, red, and black berries. What a shame it would have been had the fire destroyed them."

"I will tell the women of my village the location of these berry bushes and soon they will be offered with meals or made into jelly," Shadow Bear said.

"Jelly?" Shiona asked, her eyes widening. "Do your women truly know how to make jelly from berries?"

"Jelly and various other tasty dishes," Shadow Bear said, nodding as they now rode beside the river, the sun shining and sparkling into the water. "These bushes are called *wicakanaska,* or early berry bush."

He pointed elsewhere, to the limbs of a shrub that was growing straight up from the ground and had very small hearts, or cores. "That shrub is not from a family that food is taken from," he said. "Arrows are made from this. They are very heavy and cannot be blown away by the wind."

When he heard her inhale a nervous breath at the mere mention of arrows, Shadow Bear reached over and gently touched her arm. "The arrows used to wound my brother and that took your loved ones from you were not made from this shrub. Our Lakota hunting arrows are made with its three feathers and finished with a fluff of down that comes from under the tail feathers of a bird."

He drew his hand from her. "The two red wavering lines, the symbol of lightning, are always painted from the feathered end and halfway to the arrow tip."

Shiona's eyes widened. "That . . . design . . . was used on the arrows that downed my family," she cried.

"The two halves of the arrow that I saw in the cave were not Lakota made." He laughed throatily. "It was a poor attempt at trying to make it look as though they were Lakota, so it would look as though we had shot it."

"Then someone must be trying to black-mail your people by making it look as though one of you is responsible for these recent deaths, in addition to the wounding of your brother. Perhaps they are wanting it to look as though even a powerful Lakota chief, such as yourself, is doing this." She visibly shivered. "If this is true, then Pierre DuSault must hate you terribly for wanting to make you look guilty of shooting your very own brother," she said, shuddering visibly.

She glanced at the quiver of arrows secured at Shadow Bear's back, his unstrung bow resting over his left shoulder.

"Your arrows do not have the design you described," she said, then looked at him. "Are there many different designs used by your people?"

"Not many, but there are differences," Shadow Bear said, nodding. "The arrow I described is mainly used for hunting. That is the reason the arrow is grooved to the tip. That allows the blood to flow free from the body of the downed animal, thereby humanely hastening death."

"The arrow used on . . . on all of my family?" Shiona said shallowly. "Were they grooved to the tip? Does that mean they did not suffer all that much?"

Then her breath caught in her throat when, in her mind's eye, she saw her brother stumbling into the cave, the arrow in his body.

No. He did not die immediately.

"You do not need to answer that," she said, her voice cracking with emotion. "I . . . already . . . know."

"I see and hear your grief. But remember this, my love, your brother, mother, and father are with you always, although their flesh and bones were buried in the ground," Shadow Bear assured her. "Their spirit rides with you even now as we ride our steeds and talk."

He gestured with a wide sweep of the hand before him. "And know this, my woman," he then said. "Wisdom is all about and everywhere. There is no such thing as emptiness in the world. Even in the sky there are no vacant places. Everywhere there is life, visible and invisible, and every object possesses something that would be good forces to have, even to the very stones you see on land, and beneath the surface of the water in the river. The world teems with life and wisdom. Your family might not be there for you to see, but they are a part of that wisdom I have just spoken of."

Shiona was pleased that Shadow Bear could explain things so beautifully, especially at a time when she suddenly was missing her family so much.

Somehow she did now feel their presence all around her, and that gave her comfort and made her accept their deaths more easily.

"Thank you. Thank you for making me feel so much better about things. You are such an intelligent man. You seem to know something about everything."

Shadow Bear chuckled. "Not everything. I did not know you as deeply as I know you now. And I should have never allowed you to be alone for so long during the celebration. Had I brought you more into my activities, you would not have fled from me and placed yourself in such danger."

"It was my fault, not yours. I was so foolish," she said, her voice breaking. "How could I have ever doubted you?"

"How could I you?" he asked, reaching over and running his fingers through her golden hair. "My *hinziwin,* yellow-haired woman with violet eyes, I will never doubt you again."

A movement at Shiona's left side, in the shadows of the forest they were now riding past, made her flinch with alarm, causing Shadow Bear's hand to jerk quickly from her hair.

Although Shadow Bear was heavily armed with his bow and arrows, his powerful rifle in his gun boot, and Shiona had a rifle of her own in her own gun boot, she knew that anything could happen at anytime in this world of misplaced ideals. She knew how quickly someone could be ambushed.

"What is it?" Shadow Bear asked. He grabbed his rifle from his gun boot, his eyes peering in the same direction that Shiona was still staring.

She grabbed her own rifle when she saw

more movement close to the ground.

"Who is there?" Shiona shouted, just as Shadow Bear slapped her horse's rump at the same time he kneed his steed, in order to ride quickly from whoever might be there.

"Hurry behind that great boulder of rock," Shadow Bear shouted at Shiona, whose steed was now riding at a hard gallop alongside Shadow Bear's.

She saw which boulder he was riding toward and pointed her own steed in that same direction.

Shiona was breathless with fear, and she could not help herself but look over her shoulder to see what was happening. Her eyes widened when the culprit did quickly come out from the cover of the bushes.

CHAPTER 22

My beloved spake, and said unto me, Rise
up, my love, my fair one, and come
away.
— Song of Solomon 2:10 (KJV)

"Why, it's only several cute animals," Shiona said, relieved.

"*Iteopta-sapa,* ferrets," Shadow Bear said, smiling as he wheeled his horse around and gazed at the five black-footed creatures as they ambled away from where they had been in the bushes.

It was obvious that one was the mother, the other smaller ones, her children, which in the language of the animal were called "kits."

"I have read about ferrets, but I have never seen any up close," Shiona said, sighing with happiness that it had been nothing more than mere animals that had been causing a commotion in the bushes.

"In their own way, they are a peaceful enough animal," Shadow Bear said, still watching the ferrets as they scampered away, seemingly unaware that they were being observed, their sleek bodies arching and elongating with each of their movements. "They are so named because of their dark legs."

"They are so small, surely weighing only about two pounds and measuring two feet from tip to tail," Shiona said. "While alone in my father's study one day, after seeing a family of ferrets from afar in the nearby woods, I took one of my father's books from his library and read up on them. They were an interesting study. I discovered they are related to minks and otters. It is said their closest relations are European ferrets and Siberian polecats. Researchers theorize that polecats crossed the land bridge that once linked Siberia and Alaska, to establish the New World population."

"What I have observed of them, myself, is that these tiny animals breed in early spring when the males roam the night in search of females," Shadow Bear said, watching as the last of the ferrets bounded off and disappeared amid other bushes away from where they had first been spotted. "Mothers typically give birth to three kits in early summer and raise their young alone in abandoned prairie dog burrows."

"I read that ferrets stalk and kill prairie dogs during the night. Using their keen sense of smell and whiskers to guide them through pitch-black burrows, ferrets suffocate the sleeping prey, an impressive feat considering the two species are about the same weight," Shiona said, shivering at the thought, for to her one animal was as cute and as precious as the next. It was a shame that any had to die to sustain the other.

"In turn, coyotes, badgers, and owls prey on ferrets, whose life span in the wild is often less than two winters," Shadow Bear explained. "They have a short, quick life."

A sound, a squeak of sorts, made from the bushes from where the ferrets had come, caused Shiona's eyes to widen. She gave Shadow Bear a wondering look.

Quickly dismounting, she went to see what was causing it, knowing that whatever it was surely could not be big enough to harm her.

Curious, too, Shadow Bear dismounted and followed her.

They both stopped, their eyes wide when they saw a tiny ferret staring up at them from where it lay on the ground. When it tried to leap up, to flee, it fell back down again, and that was when Shiona saw why. Its right paw was strangely twisted and gave way when it tried to stand.

"Why it's only a baby and it was born with a lame paw," Shiona said, taken heart and soul by the helplessness of the tiny thing. "Oh, look at its masklike face and adorable round eyes."

"It has been purposely abandoned by its mother," Shadow Bear said gravely. He bent to his haunches and reached for the ferret.

When it snapped at him, he quickly drew his hand back.

"It is not used to humans," Shiona said, kneeling beside Shadow Bear. "We must gain its trust, for we cannot leave him here alone. He would surely be dead before nightfall. It would be some other animal's supper."

She looked desperately around her. "I wonder how we can get the tiny thing to trust us?" she said.

"I shall get some pemmican from my bag," Shadow Bear replied, already walking toward his horse. "I, too, feel it is not wise to leave the ferret alone, as it is so helpless. Its inability to keep up with its family is why it was left to fend for itself."

He reached inside his bag and plucked a

piece of pemmican from it, then went back to kneel beside Shiona. "This should be enough to lure the animal out," he said, slowly reaching out to place the piece of pemmican next to the ferret.

Again the ferret snapped at him, then centered its attention on that which lay close by it, its nose twitching as he slowly sniffed at the pemmican.

Then, in an instant, it had gobbled it up and seemed to beg for more as it looked into Shadow Bear's eyes.

"He liked it," Shiona said, smiling at Shadow Bear. "And he seems to still be hungry."

"I shall go for more," Shadow Bear said, soon returning with a larger portion.

They both sat and watched the tiny thing until all of the pemmican was gone. What happened next made both Shiona and Shadow Bear gasp in wonder as the ferret came out and nestled close to her, winding itself into a small ball, its eyes suddenly closed as it drifted off to sleep.

"I've never seen the like," Shiona said, slowly reaching a hand to the ferret, then gently stroking its soft brown fur. She felt the skin of the ferret ripple beneath her hand. "We must take him with us. It would be inhumane to leave him. I can't imagine its mother having so heartlessly left him."

"Survival," Shadow Bear said matter-of-factly. "Its mother was looking out for her own survival and those of her kit that were healthy enough to travel and care for themselves. This smaller, more helpless one, was slowing them down too much, which made them prey to larger animals."

"I have always wanted a pet of my own, but my father never allowed it," Shiona murmured. "He said he didn't need the bother of having one around. Please let us take him home with us. I would love caring for him and I now know how to make a lifetime friend." She laughed softly. "Food."

"It is yours," Shadow Bear said, reaching over and stroking his fingers through her golden hair.

"Oh, thank you," Shiona cried. "I could not bear thinking of leaving this tiny thing alone. I still don't see how its mother could do this."

"You are now its mother," Shadow Bear said, watching as she gently swept the ferret into her arms and held it to her bosom like she would a child of her own. "And never feel you have to ask such things of me. You are your own person. If you desire something, it is yours, without having to ask me or anyone else permission. Shame on your father that he denied you such pleasure as a pet of your own."

"My horse was all that I was allowed, but only because it was too large to take into our home, like you would a smaller animal like a dog," Shiona said, slowly standing, trying hard not to awaken the animal.

She carried the ferret to the travel bag at the side of her horse and secured him in it, leaving his face exposed to fresh air and sunlight.

"We shall name him Hope," Shiona announced.

"Hope it is," Shadow Bear said, always taken by her sweet and innocent smile when she was happy about something. It warmed his heart that he was seeing that sadness slowly fade away into the wind.

"Hope," Shiona repeated as she mounted her steed. "Yes, I do like the name, for when I look at the sweet thing, and remember how it was abandoned and was rescued, I will see the hope it has for a future that without us would have been bleak."

They rode onward beside the river. Later, Shadow Bear startled Shiona when he led his steed into the water. Horse and master swam together, with Shadow Bear's hand grasping his horse's mane.

"How beautiful," Shiona sighed, tempted

to join him, and she would have, if not for the ferret who still slept peacefully in the bag.

Her heart beat soundly inside her chest as Shadow Bear's hair became wet and clung to his powerful bare shoulders. She had never seen such a wondrous sight as this man whose eyes were as dark as all midnights as he gazed through the sunlight at her.

And then he left the water on his steed as quickly as he had entered. He dismounted and came to Shiona, water dripping from his hair onto his back and chest. She could not hold herself back any longer.

She leaped from her saddle and met him halfway, flinging herself into his arms. Everything but their yearning for each other was forgotten.

Aflame with longing, Shiona's breath quickened as she let Shadow Bear disrobe her. When she was nude in the sun's glow, she reached over and removed his breechclout as he slid his feet free of his moccasins, until he was as nude as she, and very ready for lovemaking, as witnessed by the tightness of his manhood.

"My woman," Shadow Bear whispered huskily into her ear as he urged her down onto a thick bed of moss on the riverbank.

Without further words, and with their bodies straining together hungrily, their lips met in a desperate, frenzied kiss, the spiraling need within Shiona causing her to move her body sinuously against his.

She felt her breath catch when he shoved his heat into her wet and ready place, his thrusts beginning rhythmically within her throbbing center, as she drew him farther and farther into the warmth of her body.

He held her hands above her head.

He touched his tongue to hers.

And then he moved his hands, finding the soft swells of her breasts, his lips moving, too, now fastening on a soft, pink nub, sucking gently on it.

Feeling as though she were ready to burst with the pleasure he was giving her, Shiona arched toward him, all senses yearning for the promise he was offering her.

Shadow Bear felt tremors cascading down his back, the air heavy with the inevitability of pleasure. He kissed her again, his body rhythmically moving as hers answered in kind with her own sensual movements.

Unable to hold the moment of total bliss back any longer, Shadow Bear made one last deep plunge into her, then held her hands again above her head as together they went over the edge into the total throes of ecstasy.

Moments later, they lay apart on their backs, gazing heavenward, where eagles were now soaring, some dipping lower and lower.

In an instant Shiona realized what they might be seeking. "Hope!" she cried, scurrying to her feet. She was thankful when she found him still asleep, and safe.

Shadow Bear came up next to her, swept an arm around her waist, then turned her toward him. "You already have the instinct of a mother," he said, laughing hoarsely. "That is good, for one day there will be more than a ferret for you to look after. One day, my woman, you will have a child . . . our child."

"I want nothing more than to have your child," Shiona murmured as he drew her against his powerful, hard body.

He pressed his manhood tightly against her, letting her know he was ready to make love.

"Again?" she said, giving him a teasing smile.

"Yes, but later," Shadow Bear said, chuckling.

He stepped away from her and knelt to pick up her dress.

"It is best that we return home now," he said, handing it to her and reaching for his breechclout. "I am anxious to see if my warriors were any more successful today in their search for the two evil men than they have been these past days."

"I didn't know you sent them out again today," Shiona said, combing her fingers through her hair to rid it of its tangles.

"I shall never give up searching for them," Shadow Bear said, taking her by the waist and lifting her into her saddle.

"If they are smart, they will be long gone by now," Shiona said.

She sighed with passion when he reached up and gave her a kiss on the long column of her slender neck, then swung himself into his own saddle.

"They have proven how smart they are not, by having taken on Shadow Bear," he said in a tight, raspy voice. "Too many have died." They rode off side by side.

She gazed down at the tiny animal, then at the man she would soon marry. There were two separate examples of courage . . . the courage of a powerful Lakota chief, and that of a tiny thing that was wrongly abandoned by its mother. And she loved both.

"I love you," she murmured as she gazed over at Shadow Bear and smiled, his returned smile making her almost melt with the wonder of how it was now between herself and this wonderful, handsome, and kind man.

"I shall always love you," he said back to her. "Always and forever."

"It has been a beautiful day," Shiona said, her long hair fluttering in the breeze down her back. "It is a day I shall always remember."

"We will have many more like this," Shadow Bear said, again smiling at her. "And nights. Think of the nights, my woman. It will be hard to wait for the nights to come for us to be together."

Chapter 23

Love took you by the hand
At eve, and bade you stand
At edge of the woodland,
Where I should pass.

— John Nichols

After her wonderful day with Shadow Bear, a part of Shiona didn't want to return to the Lakota village. She wished to have Shadow Bear all to herself for a while longer. But a part of her was anxious to go back, for it wouldn't be long now before they would be man and wife.

She glanced over at him and saw how his long black hair fluttered in the wind as he held his steed at a steady gallop. She never got tired of looking at him, or marveling over him.

His face was beautifully sculpted and his shoulders were so squared and muscled.

226

She smiled at how the ferret had snapped at Shadow Bear when he had first reached out for it, baring its two sharp fangs, which might have done quite a bit of damage if they'd fastened onto his flesh. But soon the ferret had made friends with them both.

She didn't see how any mother, animal or human, could be this cruel to its offspring. She could hardly wait to be a mother.

Again she gazed over at Shadow Bear. A child born of his likeness would be wondrous to behold. A son.

Yes, she hoped that their firstborn would be a son, for she had watched Shadow Bear with the Lakota children, his pride apparent even though he wasn't their father.

She knew that the young braves held the future of the Lakota people in the palms of their hands, for it was up to those young braves who would grow up to be strong warriors. They would protect the women and children so that the Lakota could grow and expand. It was their only way to be sure they were never bested by the whites who were constantly encroaching on Lakota land.

Shiona knew that there would probably be a rough time ahead, with her being a white woman married to an Indian. This might even cause her people to openly oppose Shadow Bear and his people, because they saw a marriage between a red man and white woman as taboo.

Suddenly Shadow Bear turned his eyes to Shiona. He studied her expression and knew that she had been in deep thought about something.

"What were you thinking so hard on?" he asked, sidling his horse closer to hers.

"Many things," Shiona said.

She smiled softly at him.

She didn't want to tell him exactly where her thoughts had taken her, for she didn't want him to know that she had some fear of their future as man and wife as far as the white community was concerned.

She would have to make certain she never went to trading posts with the other women. Someone else would have to do the trading for her and her family.

"What was the main thing that was causing uneasiness in your eyes?" Shadow Bear asked. "You know that you can tell me anything. We will soon be married. We should never have secrets from each other."

"I don't have any secrets," Shiona said, laughing softly. "If you must know, I was thinking about children . . . our children. I was thinking that I hope our firstborn is a son, for I know what it would mean to you." In a sense she hadn't lied by telling him only part of what she had been thinking about.

"A daughter in your image would be someone special," Shadow Bear said, his gaze steadily examining her lovely face.

She smiled at him. "Yes, I do want a daughter. You haven't said. How many children would you like to have? I've always loved children, so I would like to have at least four."

"If four children is what you want, so be it," Shadow Bear said.

Then his attention was drawn elsewhere when he spotted a lone buffalo feeding in a patch of grass a few feet away. He grew sad at how the buffalo herds had dwindled so much. Soon there would be none for his people, and he had the *washechu,* white eyes, to thank for that. Too often they had slaughtered the buffalo only because they wanted to keep the red man from having them. At times he had seen large fields of dead buffalo, killed not for their pelts or meat.

His father had seen this happening and had begun teaching the children, especially the young braves, how to live without the buffalo. Shadow Bear had continued that tradition. He watched this buffalo today with a strange pity, for it was alone, which meant that it had been separated from the others, and he hated to wonder how that might have happened.

He was afraid that perhaps not all that far away, just around the bend, where the land stretched out far and wide, some of it scorched by the recent fires, there might be a new slaughter of buffalo that he did not want to chance seeing.

So he turned his eyes away from the buffalo and rode onward, his chin held high, his heart aching for what had been, and what now was.

Shiona had seen Shadow Bear's reaction to the lone buffalo. His jaw had tightened, as had the muscles of his shoulders. Surely he had been thinking about how few buffalo were left now for the red man after men like her father, and those under his command, had purposely killed off so many.

Seeing that side of her father had saddened her so much that she had been ashamed at that moment to call him her father, for she knew the worth, even then, of the buffalo for the red man.

At that moment, a movement in the distance caught Shiona's eye. A solitary horseman was riding up against the skyline of a distant hill, leading an extra horse, which was saddled.

Panic gripped her when she identified the man as Pierre DuSault!

Had he come out of hiding long enough to capture her? Surely that was why he had the spare horse with him. Did he plan to murder Shadow Bear?

Her mind was spinning, her thoughts paralyzed by doubt and fear. She knew that Shadow Bear had surely not yet seen Pierre.

"Shadow Bear," she suddenly said. "Don't look at me as we talk. Keep looking straight ahead."

"I hear fear and apprehension in your voice," Shadow Bear said, carefully following her instructions.

"Act nonchalant," Shiona said, her hands trembling as she clutched harder to her reins.

"Why would you ask that of me?" Shadow Bear said, staring straight ahead. "Is someone near?"

"Yes," she said, her voice drawn. "It's Pierre. He's riding along the distant hill, his eyes never leaving us. And . . . and . . . he has a spare horse. Surely he is planning to steal me away from you, or at least try."

"Pierre?" Shadow Bear asked, forking an eyebrow. "After my warriors searched night and day for him? He is a man who does not

231

use his brain in a way that is normal, or he would not show his face to me or you ever again."

"Shadow Bear, don't you see?" Shiona said, her voice breaking. "We are easy targets. He has the advantage. What should we do? What can we do?"

Shadow Bear thought for a moment, then said, "We can pretend to have an argument. You can shout something at me, like you do not want me, that I am a savage, a word that all red men despise. I can ride away from you and pretend to be angrily leaving you as I ride in the direction of my village. We must look convincing to Pierre."

"But won't he shoot you in the back as you ride away?" Shiona blurted out nervously.

"No. Pierre is too far away. And he is not known to be a crack shot," Shadow Bear said tightly. "I have hunted with him. He never hit a target he aimed for."

"He surely has the bow with him," Shiona said, swallowing hard.

"Can you see if he carries a quiver on his back?" Shadow Bear asked. "Do you see a bow slung across his back?"

"He's too far away to see the arrows, but I didn't see a bow when I was looking at him," Shiona said, her fear building.

"If he does have them with him, and the bow isn't visible, that means that it is unstrung, and by the time he can string it and fire an arrow from it, I will be far enough away not to be hit by it," he said. "Pretend well, my woman. We must convince him that we are separating forever. I will go as far as I can, then circle around and kill him before he gets a chance to get to you, for I am convinced that he is here for only one reason. To have you, or why would he have a saddled horse with him? He had surely chosen one that is fast and well rested for the getaway, thinking the one you are on would be neither."

"What if he has come purposely to kill us both, not take me away with him?" she said, glancing again at Pierre, then looking quickly away again. "What if he plans to kill you and take me away, only to assault, then kill, me? We have to make certain he is killed before he gets the chance to finalize whatever his plan is."

"We must not linger any longer," Shadow Bear said. "We must get this done and over with. To delay longer might mean both of our deaths."

Although Shiona was trembling, she quickly played her part, shouting bad things at Shadow Bear; then she wheeled her horse around and rode away from him, as he did the same and rode in the opposite direction.

She then went even farther with her act than was planned. After getting what she thought was enough distance from Shadow Bear, she turned her horse in Pierre's direction.

He was already riding down the slope toward her.

She smiled, for she realized now that Pierre had taken the bait . . . hook, line, and sinker!

She began waving at him. "Pierre, oh, Pierre, please, oh, please save me from the savage," she cried. "I hate being with him and his people. I crave things I love . . . a decent bed and pretty clothes. I want you, Pierre! I was wrong not to see it earlier!"

Pierre smiled broadly at her. "My sweet! I'm coming for you. I knew you didn't want to be with the savages! I knew that you were being forced! My sweet, you will have everything. Everything! I am a wealthy man! You will be my queen!"

Her eyes widened as she thought of something. So many things had happened of late because her father had found gold. It just came to her now that Pierre had never mentioned wanting the gold!

She hoped that Shadow Bear would get there in time to save her from this man. A squeaking sound at her right side suddenly reminded her that she had more than herself to think about.

The ferret!

Surely she had not saved it only to have it killed by someone like Pierre!

She looked nervously over her shoulder for Shadow Bear, but saw no signs of him anywhere.

Pierre was so close now, she knew that if he decided to, he could shoot her. A chill rode her spine to think that just perhaps she had done everything wrong. Most certainly she had not followed Shadow Bear's plan exactly as he had said that it should be done.

"My darling Shiona," Pierre said, waving at her as he approached. "Why did you wait so long to let me know your feelings for me? I had to leave my home because of the events at Shadow Bear's village! I can explain the arrows. When I arrived home, I found them on my mule and knew they had been used to kill more than one person of late. My sweet, believe me when I say I have no idea how those arrows got on my pack mule, but they did, and I knew that you saw them and that I must flee, for how was I to know anyone would believe my explanation about them?"

Shiona's eyes widened.

Was he telling the truth about the arrows?

Had he been wrongly condemned because she had seen the arrows in his possession?

"Pierre, how do I know that you are telling the truth?" she said, drawing a tight rein and stopping as he got closer and closer.

She wasn't sure whether or not to believe Pierre!

She gazed over her shoulder, wondering where on earth Shadow Bear was. . . .

CHAPTER 24

They spoke as chords do from the string,
And blood burnt round my heart.

— John Clare

Everything seemed to change in a flash for
Shiona. Just as Pierre reached her, an arrow
sank into his chest, knocking him from his
horse. Shiona was filled with a cold dread
when she noticed the sort of arrow that had
downed Pierre. It was the same kind that
had claimed so many other people's lives.

Almost too stunned to move, Shiona
gulped and peered guardedly behind her.

Shadow Bear!

Where was he?

He had said that he would circle around
and stop Pierre before he reached her.

But he hadn't!

Then another thought came to her that
made her almost ill to her stomach.

Had he not come back to her because he had not disclosed his true plans to her?

Had Shadow Bear had the deadly arrows in his own quiver?

Was he the murderer instead of Pierre, for who else could have downed Pierre except for Shadow Bear?

She had seen no one else!

Needing answers before Shadow Bear returned, Shiona slid quickly from the saddle and knelt down beside Pierre, who was breathing hard, his eyes wild.

"Oh, Pierre, I'm so sorry. I'm confused about so many things," she cried. "When I saw the arrows on your horse that day, I thought you were guilty of having killed my family, and that you even shot Shadow Bear's brother, yet now someone shot you with the same lethal arrow. Oh, Pierre, please have enough breath left to explain things to me."

"Like . . . I . . . said, someone . . . planted . . . those arrows on my horse," Pierre said, his voice weak as death rattles suddenly rumbled through his lungs. "That is why I fled my home. I knew that I would be seen as the . . . the . . . villain in all of this."

He closed his eyes, panting for breath, then looked wild-eyed up at her. "Shiona, I . . . I . . . came out of hiding in order to save you," he said, suddenly gripping her hand. "You . . . are . . . next. . . ."

With those words, his hand dropped away and his eyes became locked in a death stare, his words suddenly silenced.

"No," she cried, mixed emotions flooding her senses. This man she thought was so evil had actually come out of hiding to try and save her. He had died trying to protect her!

"I am truly so sorry," she whispered, tears filling her eyes. Shiona rose quickly, a keen desperation grabbing at her heart.

She looked toward where Shadow Bear had gone.

"Oh, Lord, please let me be wrong," she prayed as she hurried toward her horse, her eyes still searching for Shadow Bear.

She had just reached her mount when she heard a horse coming up from behind her.

With a thumping heart she turned and saw Jack Thunder Horse ride free of the shadows of trees, a twisted grin on his face, his red hair worn in a long ponytail down his back.

"Gotcha," he said, sliding his bow across his shoulder.

He yanked his rifle from its gun boot and aimed it at Shiona's belly. "I heard your fuss with Shadow Bear and then saw Pierre riding toward you. Seems you've lost both allies this morning, one from a lover's spat, the other by my arrow."

"Your . . . arrow . . . ?" she said, gazing at the quiver of arrows with the identical design of those that had downed her family.

She was filled with a sudden guilt over having even for a few moments thought that Shadow Bear might be the one who had sent her world into a tailspin of despair.

"Yep, mine," Jack Thunder Horse said, drawing a tight rein beside her. "I bought some time for myself by planting the arrows on Pierre's steed. While the Lakota were searching for him, thinking he was the one guilty of all of the murders, I was able to stay hidden until I could find a way to get my hands on you. You see, tiny thing, taking you from him will gain me two things. I will have some fun with you while Shadow Bear searches for us; then, after you lead me to the map so that I can dig for more gold, I'll do away with you and gain the opportunity to sink one of my fancy arrows into your lover's belly."

Shiona's heart was pounding in her chest. She knew that at any moment this man's plans could be foiled, for surely Shadow Bear had already circled around and would soon be there. She just hadn't thought it would take him that long.

"You're evil, through and through," Shiona said as Jack Thunder Horse leaped from his horse and grabbed her by an arm, his rifle still in his other hand.

She winced when his fingers dug into her flesh. "How could my father have ever trusted the likes of you?" she gasped.

" 'Cause I had a likable face," he said, chuckling. He frowned. "I guess the fire took care of that, didn't it? Now I'm someone people wince at seein'."

"What are your plans for me?" Shiona asked, stalling for time.

If Shadow Bear didn't arrive soon, she would be at the mercy of a true madman!

He slid his rifle back in its gun boot, then grabbed Shiona around the waist and dragged her on his horse with him, sitting her before him with a grip of iron around her waist.

A squeak from her saddlebag drew Jack Thunder Horse's attention to the ferret, its eyes watching what was happening to Shiona.

"Well, now, what do we have here?" Jack Thunder Horse said, sidling his horse over closer to Shiona's.

He laughed throatily as he gazed at the ferret's tiny face, then laughed even more loudly when the ferret opened its mouth and snapped back at Jack Thunder Horse, as though he knew the man was evil.

Jack Thunder Horse frowned. "I've always hated those things," he said. He still held Shiona firmly around her waist, and with his free hand he grabbed his knife from its sheath. "I don't have time to take its pelt, but I will take joy from beheading the creature," Jack Thunder Horse said, reaching over. Desperate, Shiona bit his arm.

"You leave that ferret alone," she said, smiling at how he had winced with pain. "It was born disabled. Because of that it was abandoned by its mother. It deserves better out of life than what it has already been given."

"I don't have time to mess with it anyway," Jack Thunder Horse said, quickly sliding his knife back into its sheath. He grabbed Shiona by the hair and yanked her around to face him. "But one more trick like that and I'll slit your throat. Do you hear? You'll die faster than that ferret would've had I gone ahead and killed it."

Knowing that he was this heartless, knowing now that he was the murderer of her loved ones, and realizing that she was surely nothing to him but a conquest, Shiona nodded. "I won't do anything else," she murmured. "But . . . thank you for sparing the ferret's life."

"The next people to die will be you and your lover," Jack Thunder Horse said. He kneed his steed and rode off in a hard gallop toward the thick shadows of the trees. "Shadow Bear will hunt me down, and when he finds me, I'll be waiting on him. What I think I'll do is tie him up, make him watch me rape you and then kill you. Then I'll slit his throat, maybe even scalp him, and go and find the gold the map will lead me to, thanks to you."

"You're sick," Shiona said, her voice breaking. She was terrified that more talk would delay Jack Thunder Horse, which might mean Shadow Bear would fall into a trap. She stayed quiet and silently prayed that Shadow Bear would not return just yet.

Moments ago she had prayed to herself that he would arrive and save her. Now she knew that if he did arrive, he would most definitely be the next to die.

Jack Thunder Horse had gold fever. He had killed more than one person because of it, and his reign of terror seemed to have just begun!

"But now that I think of it, I don't think I have Shadow Bear to concern myself with as far as him coming for you is concerned,"

Jack Thunder Horse said, weaving his way through the thick stand of trees, heading in the direction of the cave.

"I heard your argument," Jack Thunder Horse said, chuckling beneath his breath. "And if you see Shadow Bear as a savage, surely you see me as no less, yet I am a breed. There is a difference, you know."

Shiona wanted to say, yes, there is a difference all right: One was mad, the other good, through and through.

"Yep, I'm a breed, and before I was scarred by the fire, I was a mighty handsome breed," Jack Thunder Horse bragged. "I saw you watching me at the fort. I knew then you saw something in me that you liked. But I couldn't approach you and ask you why, or your father would have made me pay for it. Yes, I kept my distance, but I had a fine time envisioning what you were like beneath those fancy clothes that you wore at the fort."

"You are disgusting," Shiona said, visibly shuddering. "If you saw me looking at you, it was because I saw in you a man my father might mistakenly trust. I see now that I was right to doubt your true worth for the fort. While you were pretending to work on their behalf, you were busy killing and maiming innocents."

"If you must know, I received much pleasure by sinking that arrow into your father's flesh," Jack Thunder Horse bragged. "Even your brother. I got sidetracked, though, by that damnable fire. Otherwise I'd have gotten the map and the gold and would be on my way to live the life of a rich man."

He reached up to her hair, grabbed hold of it, and forced her face around so that their eyes met and held. "I even saw you as a part of my plan. Not as someone to sink my arrow into, but someone who'd share the gold with me."

"And even men like you can dream, can't they?" Shiona said, laughing sarcastically into his face. "You worthless bum. I'll sink a knife into your heart at my first opportunity."

"Talk like that'll only get you in a grave much earlier than otherwise," he said, yanking on her hair.

Knowing that she had best control her temper, Shiona closed her lips tightly, relieved when he released her hair, allowing her to look away from his miserable face.

"Yep, up until now I've done everything right," Jack Thunder Horse bragged. "So far my plan has worked. I purposely placed the arrows under the blankets on Pierre's horse.

Up until he told you different, even you thought he was responsible for all of the deaths, whereas I am the one clever enough to have pulled all of this off without a hitch."

"Until now," Shiona said softly.

CHAPTER 25

Let those love now who never loved;
Let those who have loved love again.
                                    — Coventry Patmore

Completely disoriented, Shadow Bear realized that his idea had not been a good one after all. He had circled around too far and may have placed Shiona in grave danger.

His jaw tight, his eyes narrowed angrily, Shadow Bear rode onward, but having reached a bend in the path, with trees on either side blocking his view, Star reared, snorted, and tossed him from the saddle, then rode off at a hard gallop in the opposite direction.

Somewhat dazed from his hard fall, he slowly pushed himself up from the ground. He looked quickly around him and saw that his horse was nowhere in sight. Something or someone had frightened his steed so much, Star had thrown Shadow Bear, then fled the danger that surely lay ahead, just beyond the bend.

Horses were known to have a good sense of smell, and Star must have encountered something that made him flee.

Sensing danger himself, Shadow Bear cursed his bad luck, for his rifle was in the gun boot on his steed. And when he fell, his bow, which was slung across his back, had broken from the impact. The arrows had spilled from his quiver and lay around, some broken, others intact. That meant that he was weaponless except for the knife that was sheathed at his waist. And that sort of weapon could benefit him only if he could get close enough to the danger to use it.

His heart pounded. He knew how much danger he was in, and he was certain that he would not be there for Shiona when she needed him. She was probably even now with Pierre. She was at Pierre's mercy, and there was nothing that Shadow Bear could do about it.

With only a knife in his possession, he knew that his chances of living through whatever the danger was were slim.

Forging ahead, he grabbed his knife from its sheath and moved stealthily into the cover of trees at his left side.

His eyes locked ahead of him, his pulse racing, he crept onward, past one tree and then another. He knew that he was close to whatever the danger was, for he had already gone past the bend that had blocked his view earlier.

And suddenly the smell of something dead wafting toward him in the wind made him wince. He shivered from the horrible stench, then moved along.

When he came to a break in the trees, his eyes widened. He saw what had caused his horse to behave the way that it had, and now he understood.

Even Shadow Bear knew the danger he was in, for up ahead, only a few feet from him, stood a *gulo-gulo.*

His eyes widened as he recalled his grandmother's warning about wolves, how she had seen them in a vision, threatening Shadow Bear.

Ho, yes, Shadow Bear understood very well why his horse had fled after having realized the immediate danger it was in, for this animal, the wolverine, with its low-slung, stocky body, was known to fight huge animals, even as large as a moose, in order to get food for its cubs.

And this devil bear, which could locate food from a far distance with its keen sense of smell had seemed to have done just that.

Shadow Bear could tell that the carcass of the deer the wolverine was feasting on had been there for several days. Its stench was overpowering. But the smell of the dead animal, as offensive as it was to Shadow Bear, was the least of his worries.

The wolverine had brought its three cubs with her, and all four were feasting on the dead animal, seeming oblivious of Shadow Bear. He was glad that the stench of the deer was so intensely strong, for it kept the wolverine from sensing that a human was near.

Shadow Bear was careful with each move not to step on a twig, or anything that might waft in the breeze to the wolverine's keen ears. His footsteps were as light as a panther's as he backed away from the beasts.

When Shadow Bear felt that he was far enough from the wolverine, he turned and ran in the direction that he had been riding. His long hair blew in the breeze behind him. His leg muscles flexed achingly as he continued to run.

His woman.

He had not been able to follow through on their plan, and his woman was now surely with Pierre DuSault. Surely she was wondering why he had not appeared.

Shadow Bear realized now just how foolish it had been to abandon her even for one moment, although the plan had seemed workable enough. But as fate would have it at times, one's plan could go awry in the blink of an eye.

And his horse?

Where was it now?

Would it return home?

Would his warriors see it and come to his and his woman's rescue?

He only hoped that Pierre treated Shiona with respect!

If he took her far, far away from Lakota land, and he was to assault her, and Shadow Bear eventually got word of it, pity the moment that Frenchman drew his first breath on the day his mother gave birth to him!

CHAPTER 26

I was young and foolish,
And now am full of tears.
— William Butler Yeats

Filled with hopelessness, a new feeling for
he who usually had everything under control, Shadow Bear was breathless as he ran
toward the spot where he had left Shiona.
His only hope for her was that he was wrong
about Pierre's guilt.

He still found it hard to believe that Pierre was a cold-blooded murderer, because
Shadow Bear had always been proud of being a good judge of character. But at the
moment his only concern was for Shiona.

He had let his woman down!

He had foolishly left her to deal with such
a man as Pierre.

But that had not been a part of the plan!

Shadow Bear had very rarely misjudged

something, especially while on his horse and traveling along Lakota land.

For some reason today he had gotten disoriented. Nothing had looked familiar after having circled around and heading back to Shiona.

It was things such as this that made a warrior look less dependable as a chief, much less as a man!

And now his woman was in jeopardy because of his miscalculation.

He stopped for a moment to get his breath, the sun pouring down on him as he stood in the open, away from the trees. He looked cautiously around him, feeling vulnerable out in the open and at the mercy of anyone or anything that might happen along.

Especially Pierre!

"Shiona," he whispered to himself, an ache in his belly, his concern for her overwhelming. "What have I done?"

He had to chance everything now in order to try and save Shiona from the Frenchman. He had to even chance losing his own life in order to try and save hers! She had suffered already too much these past weeks. She had lost her entire white family, and surely the very man who had done this had Shiona now in his clutches.

"You will die a slow death if you hurt her," Shadow Bear whispered as he ran onward.

He ignored the pain in his legs as his muscles flexed with each stamp of his feet on the solid, hard ground as he vowed to find Shiona, no matter what lengths he had to go to to do so.

But what confused him was that he felt that he should have reached the place where he had left Shiona by now. Surely that meant that she was now truly at the mercy of the Frenchman.

And although Shiona had her own firearm with her, Shadow Bear had known not to depend on her accuracy with it. He had never known a woman who could shoot a firearm accurately enough to save a life.

He most certainly would not believe that Shiona would be that skilled with a firearm. She had grown up with everything done for her, having been protected day and night by not only one man, but an entire white people's cavalry.

Surely, all along, while Pierre had been among the Lakota people, no one had known the true measure of the man. Everyone had foolishly trusted him, among them Shadow Bear's very own grandmother, whose visions told her so much about people.

The fact that she had never seen Pierre in a vision, seeing the worth of the man, had made Shadow Bear even more comfortable as the Frenchman ingratiated himself among the Lakota people. Surely Shadow Bear, his grandmother, and all the others had been fooled by the Frenchman's jolly attitude.

Recognizing a stand of trees that stood not far from where he had been riding with Shiona, and then gazing ahead and seeing the high rise of land where he had last seen Pierre, convinced Shadow Bear that he was almost there.

Yet he had to stop and catch his breath before moving onward. He prayed to himself that his woman was still there, only seconds away, unharmed. He prayed that Pierre was with her and was ready to tell Shadow Bear how wrong he and Shiona had been not to trust him. He hoped that Pierre would have a good explanation for those arrows!

Having rested enough, Shadow Bear broke into another run.

He ran through the trees; then, when he saw a break in them a few feet away, his eyes widened and he gasped when he saw Pierre up ahead, on the ground, an arrow in his chest!

His heart plummeted to his feet, and he

felt the color drain from his face as his eyes searched desperately around for Shiona, finding her nowhere.

But . . . her horse was there!

Heartsick with guilt, Shadow Bear was at a loss as to what to do. He was grateful that Shiona didn't lie on the ground beside Pierre, a recipient of an arrow's quick death herself.

In that, Shadow Bear felt there was still a chance he could find her and save her and take her home to the safety of his village. Once he had her there, he would never put her in the face of danger again!

"I must find and save her first," Shadow Bear cried.

Risking everything in order to find his woman, knowing he was a target when he stepped free of the cover of the trees, Shadow Bear ran ahead and stepped out into the clearing, where he saw Shiona's horse, its reins hanging loose to the ground.

The steed was content to stand there and munch on some rich, thick grass, oblivious of a man lying dead a few feet away. And Shadow Bear did know now, without a doubt, that Pierre was dead.

"I was wrong about you," Shadow Bear said, falling to his knees beside the Frenchman. He reached a hand to Pierre's eyes and slowly closed them. "And I do not have time to bury you, my friend. I must leave now on my woman's horse and search for her. If only you could tell me who did this to you."

It was then that he noticed the arrow that had downed Pierre and gasped when he saw its design. It was the same that was used on the deadly arrows that had downed so many innocent people these past weeks, white and red skinned.

It did not seem to matter to the killer which he downed. It seemed that it was the pleasure the murderer got from killing that motivated him.

But today?

The killer had murdered Pierre in order to have a woman, and not just any woman, but Shadow Bear's!

He stood quickly and looked around him. "I must find him and stop him," he said, his hands curling into tight fists at his sides.

Then another thought came to him.

The ferret!

Was it still in the travel bag?

Or had it been killed, or taken?

He looked over his shoulder, along the ground, and saw no traces of the ferret, either alive or dead. Then he heard a squeaking sound coming from the bag. Smiling, he flipped the lid open, and there were the ferret's eyes peering up at him.

"And so at least you have made it through the ordeal unscathed," Shadow Bear said, daring to reach a hand out to touch the ferret, remembering how he had snapped at him the first time he had tried. He also would never forget how the animal's two fangs that stood out from all the rest of his teeth looked so sharp. But when the ferret leaned trustingly into Shadow Bear's hand, he knew that he had made a friend for life.

"I am sorry that I do not have anything to feed you, and even more sorry that Shiona is not here to love you," Shadow Bear said thickly. "And I hate to tell you, but you have a rough ride ahead of you, for I must leave now, to find my woman."

He gave the ferret a pat on the head, then closed the lid so that the animal would be more secure, and mounted Shiona's steed. He rode hard away from the death scene, in hopes of finding Shiona before anything happened to her.

He took the time to get off the horse and bend to a knee on the ground to study the tracks made by surely the assailant's horse. When he saw the direction in which they led, he remounted Shiona's steed quickly.

His eyes following the tracks, Shadow

Bear rode away from Pierre, filled with sorrow for the Frenchman who apparently had not wronged anyone.

Surely when Shadow Bear and Shiona saw Pierre, he was fleeing the wrath of the Lakota, since the arrows on his horse had made him look guilty of crimes in the area. His plan must have been to get far, far away, and had just happened upon Shadow Bear and Shiona where they usually did not ride.

He had surely had a second horse with him in order to be able to continue traveling as far as he could on one horse until it wore down, and then ride the second one until he reached safety far from Lakota land.

"I not only let my woman down, but also you," Shadow Bear sighed, thinking of the Frenchman.

A breeze suddenly stirred in the trees beside where Shadow Bear was riding and gently caressed his face. It was as though something had come and reassured him that his woman was all right, to be ready to fight for her, for soon he would be directly in the face of danger.

CHAPTER 27

Whoever loved that
Loved not at first sight?
— Christopher Marlowe

Shouts outside of Silent Arrow's tepee, where he sat with Moon Glow, drew him quickly to his feet. He hurried from his lodge, Moon Glow close behind him.

When Silent Arrow saw the cause of the commotion and shouts, he stopped, startled at what he saw.

"It is Shadow Bear's horse," Moon Glow said, stepping up at Silent Arrow's side. "But . . . where . . . is Shadow Bear? And . . . where is Shiona? They left together."

Star pawed nervously at the ground, dipped his head and whinnied softly, then raised it and shook his mane nervously.

Silent Arrow walked stiffly to Star, grabbed the reins, then studied the steed to see if there were any spatterings of blood that might indicate that his brother had been harmed. He was relieved for the moment that he saw none.

"*Mitakoza,* grandson, where is your brother?" Dancing Breeze asked as she joined Silent Arrow. "Where is his woman?"

"I have no answers," Silent Arrow replied.

Aware of the crowd that had gathered, uneasiness in their eyes, Silent Arrow stroked Star's withers and tried to remain calm.

"They must have come face-to-face with some sort of danger," Moon Glow said, her voice breaking with emotion. "Or else they . . ."

Dancing Breeze spoke up, interrupting Moon Glow. "Wolves," she said thickly. "My vision showed wolves as a threat to Shadow Bear." Tears filled her eyes. "Again my vision spoke of truth before it happened."

Silent Arrow turned to his grandmother and placed gentle hands on her shoulders. "Grandmother, what else besides wolves and my brother did you see in the vision?" he asked, searching her old, faded-brown eyes. "Did you see harm come to my brother?"

"My vision did not go farther than to see the wolves and Shadow Bear in it," Dancing

Breeze said, lowering her eyes. Then she raised them again and grabbed Silent Arrow's hands from her shoulders. She held them in a tight, desperate grip as she gazed intently into his midnight-black eyes.

"You must go and find him," she cried. "You must find Shiona. You know that for your brother's steed to return home without him can mean only one thing. Your brother, and more than likely his woman, have come to some sort of harm."

Then she dropped her hands from Silent Arrow's. "But you are not yet strong enough to search for your brother," she murmured. "You must appoint several of our most trusted warriors to go and find him."

"But *Unci,* Grandmother, besides my brother, who is the best tracker of all? I am," Silent Arrow said, proudly squaring his bare, muscled shoulders. The pucker from the arrow wound was all but gone, leaving only a slight scarring of his copper flesh.

"You are not strong enough to track," Dancing Breeze insisted, her lips narrowing in a straight line as she clamped them stubbornly together. "Appoint others. They will find Shadow Bear. They will find Shiona."

"Our most skilled trackers are out still searching for the Frenchman and Jack Thunder Horse," Silent Arrow said. "*Unci,* I must go. If not, chances are slim that my brother will be found."

Moon Glow stepped closer to Silent Arrow. "You truly must go," she said. "Silent Arrow, I know that you would not volunteer to go if you did not feel you were up to it. I have faith in you, my love. I have faith in your abilities to track and find your brother. And Shiona. They both must be found. You are the best man to do it."

Dancing Breeze gave Moon Glow a questioning stare, then reached a comforting hand to her grandson's cheek. "I, too, have faith in your abilities," she whispered. "And if you feel that you are strong enough to do this, go. Search. Find them. But beware of those who would also down you if they had the chance. Were you not already a target of someone's hate? You are fortunate the arrow did not land lower. It might have pierced your heart."

"*Ho,* I am fortunate, and I believe my life was spared because my brother would soon need me," Silent Arrow said, pride in his voice. "The spirits of my father and grandfather led the arrow to the less dangerous place in my body. They saw that I did not die because they saw the danger to Shadow Bear if I was not able to find him and bring him safely home."

Silent Arrow stepped toward the circle of warriors who were already armed, some with rifles, others with their great bows and quivers of arrows.

He looked from one to the other. "You know what is expected of us, do you not?" he shouted.

"We must find our chief and his woman!" they replied, almost in one voice.

Silent Arrow went to one and then the other, placing his hand on the shoulders of those who would ride with him, then told the others that their duties were to stay behind and protect the children, women, and elderly, especially in the absence of their chief!

Then Silent Arrow embraced both his grandmother and his woman, armed himself with weapons that would protect him, and led the pack that rode away from the village on their powerful steeds, hoofbeats on the dried earth sounding like great thuds of thunder.

Silent Arrow's eyes were keen as they watched for and followed the path that Star had come from, which should, eventually, lead to his brother. His eyes kept alert, his men following his lead.

Finally they found Shadow Bear's broken bow and scattering of arrows on the ground, which proved this was where Shadow Bear was surely thrown from his horse.

"Be careful and watchful," Silent Arrow warned as the warriors came up around him to examine the downed weapons of their chief.

"Where could he have gone?" one of the warriors questioned, his voice hollow with emotion.

"It is good that we did not find him on the ground along with his weapons, is all that I can say at this time," Silent Arrow said guardedly. "*Ho,* there is proof that he was thrown from his steed, and knowing that, we must search even more ardently until we find him."

"I see no blood, so it looks as though our chief was not wounded or harmed in any way," one of the warriors said, drawing nods from the others.

"My grandmother saw him with wolves who were threatening him," Silent Arrow said. His eyes scanned the area slowly around him, resting longer on thick brush not that far away.

His skilled eyes saw nothing lurking there, so he turned his attention to the darker depths of the forest behind them.

And then he quickly dismounted his steed. He fell to his knees and studied the tracks there, some made from Star before he bolted, and some made from moccasined feet, which he knew must be his brother's.

The absence of more prints convinced Silent Arrow that no one had assaulted Shadow Bear. What puzzled him was that he saw no prints whatsoever of wolves.

"Then what frightened Star, if not a pack of wolves?" he whispered to himself.

He moved slowly along, his eyes following the tracks made by moccasined feet, then looked quickly up at the warriors. "Follow me!" he cried as he swung himself into his saddle.

They all rode in the direction of the footprints. They rode for a long time before they saw something through the break in the trees that made them all gape in shock.

"Pierre!" Silent Arrow gasped, staring at the very man many of the Lakota warriors were searching for.

There he lay, an arrow in his stomach. That realization, that someone had died this close to where Shadow Bear had been, made Silent Arrow again feel ill to his stomach. He was afraid to look more closely around, where Pierre DuSault had fallen, afraid that he might also find his brother or Shiona.

"Who would do this?" one warrior asked.

"I am not certain, but if you look closely enough, you will see that he was downed by the same arrow that temporarily downed me," Silent Arrow said. "That means that we were wrong to think Pierre was the one who has killed so many innocent people with his deadly arrows. It is evident now that someone else besides Pierre shot the arrow into my shoulder and killed the others."

"Jack Thunder Horse . . . ," the warriors around Silent Arrow said, almost in unison, for if Pierre was not the guilty party, that most certainly left one other man who was!

And their chief, and his woman, were being stalked by that man.

"We must not waste any more time here!" Silent Arrow shouted. "We must keep searching for my brother! To delay even one more moment might mean his demise!"

CHAPTER 28

It smites my soul with sudden sickening;
It binds my being with a wreath of rue —
— Ivan Leonard Wright

Surely Shadow Bear was not that far behind, Shiona thought. He was known as a skilled tracker, so he was most likely following the tracks made by Jack Thunder Horse's steed even now.

He might be close enough that if she screamed he could hear. But she knew better than to scream. Jack Thunder Horse was violent and unpredictable. He might knock her out with the blunt end of his gun to silence her until they reached the cave.

Yes, she had to buy more time. But how? Her mind reeled with thoughts of what she might do!

She glanced at her brutal abductor's scarred features and damaged scalp, which was missing great chunks of hair. Even now some of his hair would brush her face before falling down to the ground.

She hated looking at his face.

He was hardly recognizable.

But the evil came through, reflected in his eyes. Shiona shivered with fear.

What on earth had happened to Shadow Bear? Where had he gone? Why hadn't he found his way back before Pierre had even reached her, much less before Jack Thunder Horse had time to kill Pierre, then steal Shiona away on his steed?

Then a thought came to her that made her feel suddenly ill. She paled at the thought!

Something horrible might have happened to cause his delay in returning to her.

What . . . if . . . he had also been downed by one of Jack Thunder Horse's lethal arrows before the half-breed killed Pierre?

She hung her head as tears filled her eyes. She had not thought of that possibility before, that her beloved Shadow Bear might now be lying somewhere with an arrow in his body. He would have reached them by now if he were truly still alive.

And then her eyes widened and her throat went dry when she heard something behind her and Jack Thunder Horse.

It was the sound of hoofbeats.

A horse was not that far behind them. That meant that someone was following them. And surely that someone was Shadow Bear! Shiona's heart flooded with hope.

But what if Jack Thunder Horse heard, too, and stopped to ambush Shadow Bear before he had a chance to come and save her?

Yet Jack didn't stop!

Was it possible that Jack Thunder Horse's hearing had also been affected by the fire? If so, he surely could hear only what was up close.

Wanting to help Shadow Bear in some way, Shiona desperately considered what she could do.

And then it came to her.

She smiled wickedly, then turned to face her captor.

"We don't have to go to the cave for me to get the map that shows where my father first found the gold," she said in a rush. "I studied the map. I know. All I have to do is lead you to it, if you will let me."

"If I will let you?" Jack Thunder Horse said, laughing loudly. "Why, pretty little thing, wouldn't I let you? Isn't that what this is all about? So where is it? Where should I go pan for more gold until I am the richest man in the world?"

"Richest man in the world?" Shiona said, her eyes widening. She laughed softly. *Yes, I guess someone like you would think that was what gold can get you,* she thought. She gazed more intently into Jack's eyes. "After I show you, will you let me go?" she pleaded, playing the part of a terrified maiden. She knew that if she were actually taking him to the gold, the moment he saw its glitter, he wouldn't need her anymore.

He would kill her immediately.

"Why, sure, I'd let you go," Jack Thunder Horse said. He chuckled beneath his breath. "Or better yet, we could be partners."

He leaned closer to her face, his stench making her recoil. "How's that sound?" he purposely taunted. "Wouldn't you like being my partner for life? My wife?"

"You see that stream up yonder?" she said, motioning toward it with her head. "You didn't know it, but you've been that close to the gold for some time now. I just didn't tell you."

"That stream?" Jack Thunder Horse said, his eyes widening. "The one that leads past the cave? That's where your father found his first gold?"

"Yes, the very one," Shiona said, smiling devilishly at him.

A look of triumph in his dark eyes, Jack Thunder Horse snapped the reins and turned the horse sharply left.

"Gold, I'm coming!" Jack Thunder Horse said, chuckling. "You've waited on me long enough!"

But before he reached the stream he made a sudden stop and shoved Shiona off the saddle. She landed hard on the ground, which momentarily stunned her.

"Little Miss Prissy, I don't need you anymore," Jack Thunder Horse said, chuckling. He grabbed his rifle from its gun boot and brought the blunt end down across the back of Shiona's head, rendering her unconscious.

"I lie easily," he said darkly. He slid the rifle back into the gun boot and gave Shiona a kick.

Once at the stream, he dropped his reins and fell to his knees staring hungrily into the gravel bed at the bottom of the water.

He dipped his fingers into the water and slowly and carefully began turning the rocks over, unaware of someone straightening from behind a bush, near where he had left Shiona for the critters of the night to feast on her flesh.

CHAPTER 29

She yet more pure, sweet, streight and
    fair,
Than gardens, woods, meads, rivers are.
                — Andrew Marvell

Shiona slowly awakened, her head throbbing and her eyes filled with tears. She even thought she was dreaming when she saw Shadow Bear kneeling over her.

Overjoyed, she clung to Shadow Bear's neck as he carried her quickly into the dark shadows of the forest. She laid her cheek against his powerful chest, smelling his familiar, wonderfully clean smell, feeling his muscled arms holding her endearingly close.

"I am sorry I let you down," he said as she gazed into his eyes. "I cannot explain it, but . . ."

"Shh, do not say anything," she murmured, placing a gentle finger on his lips, silencing the words she did not want to hear. "You are here now. That is all that matters."

She looked past him through a break in the trees. Jack Thunder Horse had not yet realized that she was gone and had no idea that Shadow Bear was there. What a surprise he would have! she thought merrily to herself.

"Are you all right?" Shadow Bear asked, searching her face and then her brow for signs of where the evil man had hurt her.

Shiona reached to the back of her head, gasping with pain when she found the knot there from the blow from the rifle.

"I have quite a goose egg, but other than that, I am going to be all right," she assured him. "What are you going to do now? You know that we just can't leave. Jack Thunder Horse would soon catch up with us. And when he does, let me tell you, Shadow Bear, he will be ready to kill me for what I did."

"What did you do?" Shadow Bear asked.

"I lied to him," Shiona said, giggling. "I told him that stream that he is kneeling beside is where my father found his gold. By now, surely he knows that I lied."

"But if you lied, what are those gold rocks that he has taken from the stream and is placing on the ground beside him?" Shadow

Bear asked, staring through the trees at the figure crouched by the stream.

"What . . . ?" Shiona gasped, turning around. "My word. I guess I did tell him where Father got his gold."

"But he still has not noticed that you are gone," Shadow Bear said.

He held her hands. "Stay here," he softly urged. "Be quiet. I have something to do."

Shiona nodded, then stiffened when she saw that all Shadow Bear had for a weapon was a knife.

Somehow he had lost his rifle.

She couldn't help eyeing the rifle that lay close on the ground beside Jack Thunder Horse. Lord, if he had a chance to grab it after he became aware of Shadow Bear being there, he could kill Shadow Bear before her beloved got close enough to use his knife on him.

As Shadow Bear closed in on Jack Thunder Horse, Shiona covered her mouth with her hands, her eyes wide.

She gasped when she saw Jack Thunder Horse freeze and snatch up his rifle. He spun around, but he wasn't fast enough.

Lightning quick, Shadow Bear had thrown his knife at the rifle, knocking it from Jack Thunder Horse's hand.

Jack Thunder Horse lunged for Shadow

275

Bear and wrestled him to the ground.

Shiona watched, terrified, as the two men rolled over, clobbering each other. Jack Thunder Horse momentarily got the best of Shadow Bear and started choking him. But Shadow Bear was not to be stopped that easily.

He planted a knee into Jack Thunder Horse's groin, sending him rolling over onto his back, groaning.

Shadow Bear stood up and started to reach for Jack Thunder Horse, but the half-breed rolled quickly toward the knife on the ground and tried to grab it.

Shadow Bear kicked the knife from Jack Thunder Horse's hand, and Jack crawled toward the rifle. When Shadow Bear jumped him, the gun went off, sending a blast of gunfire echoing into the air.

Shiona could not immediately tell who had been shot. Both men lay still on the ground.

She stood stock-still, scarcely breathing, as she waited, knowing that if Jack Thunder Horse was the victor, he would waste no more time on her.

He would shoot her.

Her knees buckled with relief when Shadow Bear stood up.

Jack Thunder Horse was shot dead.

Sobbing, she ran to Shadow Bear and flung herself into his arms. She clung to him; then the pair slowly walked away from the dead man.

When they reached Shiona's horse, she turned to Shadow Bear, a question in her eyes.

"I have a lot to explain, but I would like to return home first," Shadow Bear said wearily. "My people do not know if I am alive or dead. Nor do they know if you are all right. When we arrive together, we will give them double cause to celebrate and then we will have private time together. It is then that I will tell you what happened since our last good-bye."

Then he took her hands and held them tightly. "I let you down," he said gruffly. "I did not come back to you as quickly as planned."

"No, you didn't let me down," she murmured. "My darling, no one can be perfect. Even a proud chief is allowed mistakes. So please let us say no more about it. I don't need explanations. All I need is you."

She moved into his embrace. "I love you so," she murmured. "Had I lost you . . ."

"Had I, you . . . ," he said, then turned with a start when a squeaking came from the travel bag at the side of Shiona's horse.

"The ferret!" she cried, breaking away from Shadow Bear and opening the bag.

When she saw two trusting eyes looking up at her, she swept the tiny creature free of the bag and hugged it.

"Hope, how on earth did you survive all of this?" Shiona asked joyously.

"Sleep," Shadow Bear said, chuckling. "The ferret slept through most of it and is better for it."

"I'm so glad," Shiona said, clutching the tiny animal to her bosom. "He has already suffered enough."

"Let us take him home," Shadow Bear said, nodding.

"Yes, let's," she said, sliding the ferret back into the bag.

Just as they stepped free of the shadows of the forest, they saw Silent Arrow leading several warriors toward them.

"My brother!" Silent Arrow cried as he dismounted beside Shiona's horse.

"My brother, you were strong enough to ride?" Shadow Bear asked, his eyes moving slowly over his brother. He smiled and patted Silent Arrow on the shoulder. "*Ho,* I see that you are."

"I could not stay home while others came looking for you," Silent Arrow said, his voice drawn.

"I know," Shadow Bear said, placing an arm around his brother's muscled shoulder. "But now we can all go home. All is fine."

Silent Arrow looked past him and saw Jack Thunder Horse dead not far from the stream, and then he spied the gold pellets that lay on the ground nearby.

"That man was gold hungry," Silent Arrow said thickly. "So much that he died for it."

"I will go for his horse," Shadow Bear said, glancing over his shoulder at Shiona. "My woman, you can have your steed now. I shall have Jack Thunder Horse's."

Shiona nodded, smiled, then swung herself into the saddle, eager to reach home at last.

CHAPTER 30

How many days, thou dove,
Hast thou been mine?

— Barry Cornwall

As Shiona entered the village with the others, she immediately saw Dancing Breeze and Moon Glow standing with the crowd, relief obvious on their faces.

Before Shadow Bear could even dismount, Dancing Breeze was beside his horse, waiting, tears spilling from her eyes.

Moon Glow took her place beside Silent Arrow's steed, her own tears proof that she had been afraid that something might happen to her beloved again, and this time he might not be as fortunate.

"My grandson," Dancing Breeze cried as Shadow Bear dismounted and pulled her endearingly into his arms. "What delayed your return? Was it as my vision warned?

Was it wolves?"

Shadow Bear was momentarily at a loss for words. He wasn't certain what he should tell his grandmother. It did not seem right to have to tell her that she was wrong, that her vision had not turned out to be as she had said it would be, that there were no wolves, but instead wolverines that had caused his steed to throw him. He was reluctant to point out her mistake, for what would that accomplish?

"*Ho,* wolves," he said, knowing that only he would ever know that truth. "They frightened my horse. Star threw me."

"I am so sorry," Dancing Breeze said, stepping away from Shadow Bear. She placed a gentle hand on his face. "But I am so glad that the wolves did not attack you and take you from me and our people."

She went to Shiona and embraced her. "And how have you fared during this time of danger?" she asked softly.

"As you see, I am fine," Shiona said, trying to ignore the throbbing of the lump on the back of her head.

There was no need to get into a lengthy dialogue with Dancing Breeze about what had truly happened.

She would leave the telling up to Shadow Bear.

Whatever he thought needed saying, he could say it.

"Everyone is fine," Shadow Bear said, smiling around at his people, seeing keen relief in their eyes now that he was finally home among them, safe.

He went to Shiona and gathered her in his arms. "The two men who were hunted by our warriors are now dead," he said. "But I must tell you that the one we have enjoyed so much among us during our celebrations turned out not to be the one who wronged us. Pierre was blackmailed by the one who was guilty. He was also killed by him. The villain who wronged us more than once is none other than Jack Thunder Horse, the man who turned his back on his true people and became a scout for the *washechu* pony soldiers. He was blinded by greed, by his hunger for the white man's gold rocks. But he will no longer cause anyone any heartbreak by his wicked, greedy, misguided ways. He lies dead beside the gold rocks that in the end caused his demise."

One of Shadow Bear's warriors who had stayed behind to guard his people in the absence of his chief and so many trusted warriors stepped forward. "It is good to know that Pierre was not evil," he said gravely. "We gave him trust."

"Well-deserved trust," Shadow Bear said. "And because of this, several of you must return to where he now lies and recover his body. He deserves a proper burial."

Several warriors nodded.

Shadow Bear appointed one of the men who had ridden with Silent Arrow and knew where Pierre had fallen to lead the others. Then he hugged Shiona even closer and said, "I have learned many lessons these past weeks and most important of them is that sometimes there is no tomorrow, that someone can steal it away as quickly as one can blink an eye. I also have chosen the woman who will be my wife and who will bear me children. We will marry soon."

"As will I marry Moon Glow," Silent Arrow suddenly announced, as he smiled at Moon Glow, who stood beside him. "We have waited too long as it is."

He gazed into her eyes. "Will you be my wife?" he asked.

"*Ho,* I will be your wife," Moon Glow said, smiling sweetly up at him.

Shadow Bear took both of Shiona's hands in his. "And will you marry me soon?" he asked, searching her eyes.

"Yes, oh, yes," she said, holding back tears that were burning at the corners of her eyes, happy tears, tears of joy. "I will cherish you forever and ever. I will be proud to be your wife. I will be happy to bear your children. They will be born of our love."

"I will cherish you always," Shadow Bear said, his voice drawn with emotion. "I promise never to let anything or anyone hurt or threaten you again. I do want you, *mitawin,* my woman. When you marry me you will not only be my wife, but a part of my family of people, who are as one with me, and who will be as one with you. I promise that you will never be afraid or lonely again."

She flung herself into his arms as everyone cheered and clapped.

Then she remembered the ferret.

She hurried to her travel bag and removed it, the sight of the tiny animal drawing many gasps from the children.

One child in particular, who had recently lost both parents, and who now lived with his grandparents, stepped forth. He reached a hand out to the ferret and pet it. When Shiona saw that the ferret did not snap at the child, but instead allowed him to pet it, she handed the ferret to the eight-year-old boy.

"His name is Hope," Shiona said sweetly. "Would you like to have it as your own?"

"You are giving the ferret to me, to keep?"

Two Eagles gasped.

"If your grandparents approve," Shiona said.

She watched him run over to his grandparents, and tears filled her eyes when they, too, petted Hope.

When they nodded to him, giving their permission, and Shiona saw the joy that this brought into the child's eyes, she knew that she had done the right thing.

He ran back to Shiona. "I can have him," he said, his eyes gleaming with happiness.

"Then Hope is yours," Shiona said, reaching a hand to his thick, dark hair, tousling it playfully.

"Thank you," Two Eagles said, then ran toward a gathering of children his own age, giving each a turn petting Hope.

Shadow Bear pulled Shiona into his arms. "You are a woman of good heart. What you did will bring the child happiness inside his heart that was stolen away when renegades killed his parents."

He bent low and whispered into her ear. "Come with me." He took her by the hand and led her away from the crowd.

They ran toward the river. "It is time to wash the stench of everything we have encountered today from our bodies," Shadow Bear said over to her. "And then I have other plans for us both."

Shiona was breathless when he stopped, turned, and swept her into his arms, then ran on with her until they reached the river. They ran alongside the water until Shadow Bear found the privacy he wanted and he carried her into the water.

Giggling, Shiona kicked her feet and playfully splashed water onto his face. He released her and they swam side by side, their laughter lifting into the wind, the sun almost lost from view as it dipped low behind the thick forest.

After a short while, Shadow Bear stopped and held her in his arms, his eyes devouring her. "I think it is time for us to return to our lodge," he said warmly. "I want to show you the way I make it up to my woman for having let her down."

"You didn't let me down," Shiona whispered. "You could never let me down. Never."

She trembled with ecstasy as he rained kisses across her brow, down her cheeks, and then her lips.

Then he swung her up into his arms and carried her from the river and on to their home.

After he secured the ties at the entrance-way, he turned to her and held his hands out for her.

"Come with me to our bed," he said.

She smiled, took his hands, and went with him to the thick pallet of furs and blankets.

After disrobing her, he let her remove his wet breechclout and moccasins, and then he pulled her into his embrace, and with his body gently eased her onto the bed.

She clung to his shoulders and leaned her body more tightly against his, ecstasy moving in with bone-weakening intensity when he softly nudged her legs apart, then with one great shove, entered her and filled her with his heat.

He surrounded her with his hard, strong arms and crushed her to him so fiercely, she gasped.

His body, his mouth, were sensuous, hot, and demanding.

Her body was yearning for the promise of what he offered, as a frantic passion now claimed her, body and soul.

She clung to him.

He clung to her.

They rocked together.

They rolled over, so that she was now on top, and then as quickly she was on the bottom again, the recipient of his heated thrusts, which came to her more intensely now, so much that she could feel the urgency between them building.

He again gazed into her eyes, as she devoured him with her own.

Then she moaned with ecstasy as he slid his mouth down and locked his lips over the tight nub of one of her breasts, his teeth nipping, his tongue lapping.

She threw back her head in a frantic passion, breathing so hard, her heart could hardly keep up.

When her head began to reel, she knew that the most exquisite of feelings was drawing near, when they would reach that pinnacle of passion together.

Her blood surged in a wild thrill as she locked her legs around his waist, riding with him now, thrust by thrust, as she lifted herself to receive him.

Then she melted into a wondrous surrender, a sweetness only lovers knew, overwhelming her once again. She sighed against his lips as he came to her once more with an explosion of kisses, his arms locked around her so tightly that when he moved, she moved with him, as though they were one entity.

Breathless, Shadow Bear smiled down at her, stroking her cheeks with his fingertips. Then his hand moved down to curve over her breast, bringing out a sigh of pleasure from deep within her as she smiled down at what he was doing. His skin quivered with the need to fill her deeply again with his heat.

His arms snaked around her and brought her tightly against him once more; then he slid himself inside her with a hard plunging of his heat, his loins aflame. And they both found that place of wondrous release and passion together.

After they had reached that wondrous moment, they lay quietly together, their pulses racing, their hearts beating in unison, as though they were one.

Her breasts pulsed warmly beneath his fingers as he caressed one and then the other.

"Your body was made for loving," he said thickly, leaning over to flick his tongue over a nipple. "You will never need ask for it. I will always be there for you, to offer it."

Dancing Breeze's voice from outside the closed and secured entrance flap tore them suddenly apart, their eyes wide, their breathing rapid.

"I know that I am flushed from lovemaking. Surely she will notice," Shiona said as she reached for a dress that lay not that far from where they had made love.

She slid it over her head and combed her

fingers through her hair, as Shadow Bear dressed as quickly in a dry breechclout, his hands as eager in his own hair.

"My grandmother was young and in love herself and knows that when a woman and man are together in a lodge where the ties are secured, they are more than likely making love," Shadow Bear said.

He went to Shiona and smoothed some hair in place, as she did for him, too. Then he went to the entranceway and soon had it untied and was holding it back for his grandmother to enter.

"I have brought something special for Shiona," Dancing Breeze said, hiding a smile.

She had had her days, weeks, months, and years of such pleasuring.

But now her husband was gone.

She was old.

And lovemaking was for the young.

"What is it?" Shadow Bear asked.

In response, Dancing Breeze held out a dress for Shiona.

Shadow Bear was pleased, but what confused him was that it was not a newly made dress. He could see how the white feathers on it had yellowed with age. As had the doeskin that the dress had been made from yellowed.

Dancing Breeze turned to Shiona.

"Shiona, woman that my grandson will soon marry, will you please this old woman by wearing the very dress that she was married in?" she said, her voice soft and lilting as she smiled into Shiona's eyes.

Shiona was deeply touched.

The dress was feather-trimmed, the feathers that were once as white as a new-winter snow, aged and yellow, but no less lovely.

The dress was also quilled, beaded, and fringed.

"You truly will allow me to wear this beautiful dress?" Shiona murmured, taking it gingerly from Dancing Breeze.

"I have never seen so lovely a dress," Shiona said, tears filling her eyes.

"And, yes, *ho,* I will happily wear it. I . . . I . . . will feel so special while exchanging vows with my beloved Shadow Bear. Wearing your dress will make our day one that will be even more cherished."

Shadow Bear was well pleased. It was wonderful to behold how his grandmother, who had seen many bad things done their people by the *washechu,* white man, had taken Shiona into her heart and loved her as though she were born into their people's lives.

"Shiona," Dancing Breeze said, reaching a

leathery hand out and gently touching Shiona's cheek. "You are different from any white people I have ever known. Woman of my *mitakoza*'s, grandson's, heart, I do not look to you as white, for you have proved time and again that you are nothing like the *washechu* that have become a thorn in my people's sides. Shiona, sweet Shiona, somewhere in time you became Indian; you are Indian."

Shiona's eyes widened and she gasped with wonder. To have heard this elderly Lakota woman, the grandmother of the man Shiona adored and would soon marry, honor her in such a way meant the world to her.

"How can I thank you enough for what you have just said?" Shiona said, sniffling as she fought back the urge to cry tears of pure happiness. "I am so honored. Thank you so much for this honor, this pure joy, Dancing Breeze."

"You made it so because of who you are and how you are among my Lakota people, who are, in truth, now yours," Dancing Breeze murmured.

"Thank you, Grandmother," Shadow Bear said, gently drawing her into his embrace. "What you did for my woman, and for me, surpasses any words I can offer. I cannot find words enough to tell you how much you are appreciated and loved."

"I am only one little old lady," Dancing Breeze said, leaning away from him and smiling into his majestic, midnight-dark eyes. "My *mitakoza,* all I have ever wanted for you is your happiness, and since Shiona has became a part of your life, I have never seen such happiness in your eyes. I am happy for you."

Shiona gingerly placed the dress on their bed; then all three of them hugged at once, their joy filling the lodge with an abundance of warmth and light!

Chapter 31

With tongues all sweet and low,
Like a pleasant rhyme,
They tell how much I owe
To thee and Time!

— Barry Cornwall

Moon of Making Fat — June
Summer heat blanketed the woodland and river. Several years had passed and as Shiona and Shadow Bear walked, they remembered the wonders of their lives as man and wife.

As Shiona gazed at the patterns of lichens and moss on the rocks along the shoreline, she could not help but remember the shine of gold that had lured her father into a fate that had changed everything for his family.

Especially Shiona.

She was happier than it seemed possible

to be. She and Shadow Bear had had two children. One was a son, born of his father's image, with copper skin, midnight-dark eyes, and long black hair.

The other was a daughter, also born in her father's image, except for one difference . . . she had her mother's luscious violet eyes!

The names they had chosen for their two children were not altogether Indian. Because of their daughter's eyes, she had been named Violet, which was also Shiona's grandmother's name.

Their son's name had been chosen because of how many eagles had come that day, soaring in the wind just as Shiona had been giving birth. He was named Wind Eagle.

"See how the stones in the river bed look like otters at play?" Shadow Bear asked, taking her hand and stopping her.

They both gasped when they noticed the shine of gold there also. They then looked over at each other and laughed.

"Today our children, with Silent Arrow and Moon Glow's two sons, are along the river, somewhere behind us, each racing their ponies," Shadow Bear then said.

"Violet is almost as skilled at riding as are the boys," Shiona said, smiling over at

Shadow Bear as he turned his eyes to her. "Are you not as happy, my husband?"

He paused, then chuckled. "*Ho,* I am as happy," he said. Then his eyes became sad with a thought other than children. "I wish my grandmother were here to see the children," he said thickly. "That day, after our wedding, she went to her bed and fell asleep and never woke again."

"But she went to join her husband in the sky, and all others who went on before her. The smile on her face as she lay there, so beautiful in her best dress, proved that she had met with her husband and was even then walking, hand in hand, amid the sunflowers," Shiona murmured.

"One cannot ask for more than that when they lose a loved one," Shadow Bear said, nodding.

He stopped and reached for Shiona and drew her into his arms. "You are happy, are you not?" he asked, searching her eyes.

"How can you ask that?" She twined her arms around his neck. "Let me show you just how happy I am."

Their kisses came together, sweet and joyous, the world around them newborn with lovely flowers, trees, and tall, rich and green grass, having won the war with that horrible devastating fire those years ago.

Again, the land of the Lakota could be described as paradise, except for the whites who still crowded the Lakota.

But even though the Lakota had that to live with, and accept, their lives were good, their people, happy!

Dear Readers:

I hope you enjoyed reading *Shadow Bear,* the second book of my new Dreamcatcher Indian series, which I am writing exclusively for Signet. The third book of that series will be *Falcon Moon,* and it will be on sale in January 2008.

Those of you who are collecting the books of my Dreamcatcher series and want to hear more about it and my entire backlist of Indian books, as well as my fan club, can send for my latest newsletter and an autographed bookmark.

Write to:

Cassie Edwards
6709 North Country Club Road
Mattoon, IL 61938

You can visit my Web sites at:

www.cassieedwards.com, or
www.myspace.com/cassieedwardsromance

Thank you for your support of my Dream-catcher series. I love researching and writing about our country's very first people!

Always,
Cassie Edwards

CASSIE EDWARDS

After my children were grown, I found myself restless, searching for ways to busy my idle hands and mind. I discovered my love of writing, and I was drawn to the mystique of Indian lore. What I learned about the Native American people inspired me to bring their stories to life through the wonderful genre of historical romance.

Having lived in St. Louis for thirty years, my husband and I returned to Mattoon, Illinois, when he retired from teaching. My dream house is peaceful and quiet, where an occasional curious red fox ventures onto my sundeck and peeks into my office, and where I can watch swallows building their nest and raising their babies right outside my kitchen window. It is the perfect place to create my novels.

I feel blessed to have found a "second life," the first having been spent raising two happy and healthy sons. Writing my Indian romances is my small tribute to those beautiful first people of our land who have suffered so much injustice. And I have just begun. My upcoming books will continue with more passion and adventure and rich historical settings. Enjoy!

We hope you have enjoyed this Large Print book. Other Thorndike, Wheeler, and Chivers Press Large Print books are available at your library or directly from the publishers.

For information about current and upcoming titles, please call or write, without obligation, to:

Publisher
Thorndike Press
295 Kennedy Memorial Drive
Waterville, ME 04901
Tel. (800) 223-1244

or visit our Web site at:

www.gale.com/thorndike
www.gale.com/wheeler

OR

Chivers Large Print
published by BBC Audiobooks Ltd
St James House, The Square
Lower Bristol Road
Bath BA2 3SB
England
Tel. +44(0) 800 136919
email: bbcaudiobooks@bbc.co.uk
www.bbcaudiobooks.co.uk

All our Large Print titles are designed for easy reading, and all our books are made to last.